THROUGH THE DOG'S EYES

A LOVE STORY

SAL SANFILIPPO

Copyright © 2022 Sal Sanflippo
All cover art copyright © 2022 Sal Sanflippo
All Rights Reserved

This is a work of fiction. Names, places, characters and incidents are either the product of the author's imagination or are used fictitiously, and any resemblance to any actual persons, living or dead, businesses, organizations, events or locales is entirely coincidental.

No part of this book may be reproduced or transmitted in any form or by any means, electronic or mechanical, including photocopying, recording, or by any information storage and retrieval system, without permission in writing from the author.

Publishing Coordinator – Sharon Kizziah-Holmes

Paperback-Press
an imprint of Paperback Press, LLC.

ISBN -13: 978-1-956806-84-7

DEDICATION

To my family, past and present, who helped show me the way, and to the dogs I've loved who've joined me on the journey.

ACKNOWLEDGMENTS

I owe a tremendous debt to my intrepid writing group. Their skillful eyes joined this neophyte author through the maze of dangling participles, passive voice, cliches, and filtered narration to write what I hope is a story many will enjoy: TJ Orr, Norma Sadler, Bill Preston, Darrell Clausen, Joe Beaver, and Jim Adams. Special thanks to my beta readers Cathy Feldman, Terry Weed, and Brandon Boelter.

I also must recognize the dogs who ran by my side as a boy, later sat at my feet as I wrote, or raced beside me on this joyful journey through life: Butch, Brownie, Pepper, Terry, Phoebe, Captain, Maeve, Lola, Blake, Pup, Tootsie, Poseidon, Yuki, Kira, Matilda, Harley, Diego, and DK. I love you all.

Mom, thank you for always believing. And lastly, my incalculable debt to my loving wife, Gina, and children, Michael and Leah, who fill my life with meaning.

PART I

The Boy

Something is calling, pulling me away from the boy I love, the boy who has been my life. I struggle against the call's powerful tug. I can't go. No, not yet. I'm not ready.

I fight to keep my tired eyes from closing. I'm frightened, not for me but for the boy. I have always been there for him, but I fear I must go. My part in his story is coming to an end. My eyes flicker, and the memories of our time together rush toward me. They are bright, lighting the way for the journey I must take, warming my soul with reminders of the love we shared.

The lights pull me back to the beginning, so long ago. I surrender, and the memories engulf me. Perhaps the welcoming lights will know. Is he ready? Have I done enough?

I close my eyes, remembering the first time I ever saw My Boy.

I was in a large box lined with old towels, wrestling and playing with the others, as someone new entered the house. I stopped, sniffed deeply, and cocked my head as several humans walked into the room. They smiled, making those noises I'd heard humans make. Noises, I came to learn, were their way of communicating. Humans aren't as smart as dogs and often need to yammer away like frightened pups, yapping and yipping to get their point across. The humans looked down at us, pointing, smiling, and making those noises.

Next to the nice lady who'd been helping our mother with her large litter of pups stood several new humans: a lean, powerful man with hard, demanding eyes, a kindly-looking woman, and a special boy who was to become my own. I liked the smell and look of the boy immediately and wanted him to pick me up.

I stepped on my sister's head and nipped on the ear of one of my brothers to move him out of the way. Then, with my front paws scratching on the side of the box, I looked up to see the larger humans. Their eyes flashed, moving from one puppy to the next. But the boy's eyes fixed on me and never turned away.

He had hair blacker than night and bright, dark eyes that held my gaze in a way no human ever had. Our eyes locked, and it was like I had known him all of my life, even longer, if that were possible. I shivered with excitement as he reached into the box and picked me up to hold me to his chest. He smiled, warming my heart.

I was home.

People had visited and played with us over the last few days, ultimately taking two of my sisters away, never to return. I'd watched my siblings act excited and cute, but I hadn't been interested until the boy picked me up. Oh, I behaved. I didn't deliberately pee on anyone or nip. But until he picked me up, I wasn't sure why I had no interest in leaving with any human. Now I understood. I'd been waiting for this boy. I had to go home with him. He needed me, and I had to be there for him.

I didn't have to embarrass myself. The boy brought me close as I licked his hands and face. He tasted like he smelled, healthy and gentle, with an inner strength that would draw people to him his whole life. It was a strength that drew me to him and one he would desperately need in the years to come. The boy didn't pull away or giggle. He accepted the licks, and his smile grew. Then he turned to the other humans and spoke.

"He's the one."

It's strange, until that moment, all the noises humans made were gibberish to me. But once the boy spoke, it was like early morning when the woman helping my mom would come into the room where we slept, touch a spot on the wall, I'd hear a click, and my world lit up like going out in the midday sun.

Suddenly, I understood humans' noises as words, or at least the boy's: *Good dog . . . Don't . . . Let's walk . . . Come here . . . I love you.* In the coming days I would discover a whole new language and a boy of my own to share it all with.

My Boy.

He held me close and walked out of the house into an icy-cold clear daylight. Shocked by the biting cold, I nuzzled against his warm body as he carried me away from the only life I'd ever known. Something roared high above us, and he stopped. My Boy stared up into the sky as a giant shiny bird raced across the clouds. His chest beat faster, matching my pounding heart, and his eyes flashed in excitement like he'd found his favorite toy to chew. His eyes grew wider, and he held me closer, our hearts now beating as one.

"That's gonna be me someday, buddy. Just you wait and see."

I would see that look and hear the excitement in his voice a lot in the years to come whenever he stared into the sun-streaked sky. My Boy wanted something special out of life, and I was to be by his side as he chased his elusive dreams.

Coming Home

I was in heaven. I'd gone to live with My Boy and the two bigger humans I learned were his mother and father. I'd never known my father. Yet I sensed my mother's job, looking after a litter of helpless, blind pups, then later energetic balls of fury roaming everywhere, would have been easier if our father had been with us. But he wasn't around to offer a watchful eye, a gentle nip to behave, or to pick us up in his mouth by the scruff of our necks to carry us back when we strayed too far. Sadly, I was to see the same come to pass for the boy, but I'm getting ahead of myself with our story.

My Boy was called Jake, and I loved hearing his name.

"Jake will be home soon, and he can take you for a walk."

"Jake, when you finish your chores, you can play with the puppy."

"Yes, Jake, the puppy can sleep in your bedroom."

Every time I heard his name, good things happened.

His parents had several names. Mostly they were Mom and Dad, but some people called them Anna and John, or sometimes Gio.

That first night in my new home, I missed the warmth of my mother and siblings. But Jake put me in a small box lined with a soft blanket and brought me into the room where he slept. He lay on the floor next to me, his hand resting inside the box. In time, his gentle breathing calmed me, and I fell asleep to the sound of his soft, welcoming murmurs.

Frightened in the night, I yelped and opened my eyes to search for my mother, only to see Jake looking down at me and smiling. I moved closer. Instead of my mother and the nice lady, I had someone new who'd be there for me. With the feel of his soft touch, I closed my eyes and fell back into a deep sleep.

Most mornings, Dad left the house to go someplace called the station house. He'd wear the same clothes each day, clothes I learned were a part of his uniform. After playing with me almost my entire first day home, Dad went to the stationhouse, and Jake went to someplace called school. I whimpered at first. Why did he have to go to school? Why couldn't I go to this school place with him? I knew if given his choice, Jake would take me. But no, my responsibility was to stay home and help Mom not be so sad.

Mom moved slowly, like she'd been hurt, and would pick me up to hold me in her lap before dropping her head to cry. I'd lick her face, and her tears would stop as she softly smiled. I'd done my job. I'd helped chase her sadness away. In time,

Mom went back to something they called teaching, and I was left alone. But in those early days, while she was getting better, she stayed home so I could look after her and help her get happy again.

Mom watched me skidding on the slippery floors in the house, chasing the ball she rolled from room to room. My thick tail whipped back and forth while Mom giggled and called me her "furry godsend."

We were all coming together, learning about each other, and building a life, something wonderful as we grew to know and understand the others' needs. I loved them all, but the highlight of my day was the time I spent with My Boy. I waited for Jake to come home. Our connection was special, and our story would be the most meaningful one of all.

Each day my understanding of the bond we all shared grew. I followed Jake everywhere, watching him and his parents work around the house. I heard the word *family* a lot, my tail thumping briskly. I was now a part of this thing they called family. When I was with my mother and siblings, suckling and exploring that box and small room, I was part of a pack, but this was different. This was better. It was forever. This pack, this family, would be mine for all time, and my job was to love them, protect them, and make them proud.

Loving and protecting them came naturally. Love poured out of me like rain from a cloud-filled sky, and protecting them, well, that was just so natural. I barked every time I heard a strange sound. I knew they'd want me to warn them of this new presence near our home. Although still very young, I was growing quickly. Dad often looked at my paws and talked about how big they were. He said that meant I would be a *big boy*. Everyone laughed as Mom told them, with my size and constant barking, I would become a great watchdog. I didn't know what this meant, but if they were happy, so was I, and I'd do anything to earn their love and to protect them.

But at first, I struggled with the making them proud part. I quickly learned my family would be disappointed if I did my *business* anywhere other than outside or on the papers placed on the floor in the small room where they kept their boots and the balls and sticks Jake played with. I'd hear "Good boy" when, after a long wait, I'd go outside to do my business.

Yes, it was the other rules, those *make them proud* rules, I had to learn. I didn't understand these rules, and that was about to get me in big trouble.

After a few days in my new home, they left me alone for the first time.

I panicked. They put me in the small back room and pushed boxes in front of the entrance to block the way to the rest of the house. They thought this would keep me out of the other rooms.

They didn't know me that well yet.

Bad Dog

A door closed, and I heard a car start. For the first time in my life, I was alone. Frightened, I whimpered, searching for a way out of the back room where they'd blocked me in, but my emotions quickly turned to anger. How could they do this to me? Hadn't I already shown them I loved them? Hadn't I shown I would protect them, and still they left me alone?

I barked furiously and tore at the boxes with my paws and teeth until one of the smaller boxes tumbled down onto the ground in front of me. I jumped on top of the box, which allowed me to jump onto another box and the next. Then, at last, I jumped down to the floor outside the room to freedom and what I later heard my humans call *the complete run of the house.*

Delighted to be out of the small room, I raised my nose to sniff the air. There was no sense looking for my family. I'd heard the car drive away. Although still scattered throughout the house, their smell was older, lacking its usual freshness. They were nowhere nearby. My tail high, I looked around, my fear and anger fading.

Yes, to be away from my family could be scary, and I'd been angry to think they'd do this to me after all the love I'd shown them, but those feelings slipped away, replaced by something new and exciting. I was alone, away from my brothers and sisters, away from my humans. For the first time in my life, I was completely free. I could go anywhere I wanted, sniff anything I wanted, climb on anything, play with anything, chew on anything, and yes, *eat anything* I could find!

I admit, I didn't think through my first exposure to freedom. Still young and filled with energy, I reveled in my independence and probably made a few mistakes. Delighted to be out of that room, I wanted to play.

Racing around our home, I entered a big room where I hadn't been allowed before. A tall tree stood in the corner with brightly stacked boxes surrounding it. The tree had shiny balls hanging off the branches, and that corner of the room smelled much different from the other rooms. I'd never seen a tree in a house before, but I knew balls were for playing, so scampering up over the boxes, I tugged at the balls with my fiercest growl as I tried to pull them from the tree. One of them broke into several sharp pieces in my mouth, which I carefully spat out. After that, I only used my paws to attack the balls while I continued trying to knock them from the tree.

I'm not quite sure how, but at one point, my paw caught on something shiny wrapped around the tree. I tugged franticly to escape, and the entire tree began to sway. Then it attacked, landing on top of me. My paw now free, I crawled out from under to freedom.

With my tail between my legs, I trembled, frightened by the unexpectedly crashing tree. But the sight of all those balls rolling across the floor made me forget my little scare. Head high, I ran after the shiny balls. Then, with one of the smaller prizes now securely captured and filling my mouth, I trotted back to the fallen tree.

I dropped the ball, my eyes widening as I spotted a flat box, already open, with a fluffy piece of cloth resting inside. Filled with energy and enjoying my freedom, I pounced on the cloth and tore at it with growling excitement. I snapped my head back and forth, relishing the instinctive urge to tear open this thing locked between my teeth. My growl deepened as long-forgotten memories of hunting and capturing animals in the wild called to me and I surrendered to the urges.

I paused, the shredded cloth hanging from my tightly clenched teeth. Maybe I shouldn't be tearing things up. But it was so much fun. Besides, I hadn't completely forgotten my anger at being left alone. I figured it might be good to show my family how much better their life could be when they were with me, so I played on.

In time, I tired of these games, and my stomach made a familiar sound. I knew what that meant. Time to eat.

Sliding across the cool, slick floor, I ran to the room where we ate every night. I took a long, sloppy drink from the water bowl Mom and Jake always filled for me. But the other bowl, where they put my food each night . . . Empty. My nose twitched. There was food nearby. I moved on to explore.

Most of the family's food was kept behind doors or up high, far above any area I could reach. But I saw the countertop lined with all types of foods, offering different and wonderful aromas. The smell of fish, meat, and all kinds of sweet treats tickled my nose, and my ears perked at a curious scratching sound. Everything shouted out to me: Come and explore!

I jumped up on my back legs, but my paws couldn't even reach the top of the counter, never mind trying to get my nose near any of the wonderfully delicious aromas. I'd never get to the food or discover the odd noise that way, so I continued to explore. Then, I noticed the small stool Mom stepped on when she needed to put things away high up in the cupboards. If I could get on top of it, maybe I could get to the food. So I scrambled up onto the stool. My body trembled, standing high on my back legs, pawing at the counter, and I almost turned back. But I was so close. I could smell all those wonderful aromas. I couldn't give up.

Back with my brothers and sisters, I was always the one to roam the farthest, potentially suffering a quick nip on my bottom from my mother or a jealous snap at my ear from one of my brothers. The reproach might cause me to pause, but it never stopped me for long. It made me proud knowing I didn't frighten like the others and that I wouldn't quit easily. I'd continue to push on when my brothers or sisters might turn back. After all, wasn't that how I got Jake to notice me the day he picked me to take home with him? I wouldn't have found my wonderful family if I let little things like a nip from one of my siblings or the fear of a fall frighten me.

In my new home, I told myself nothing should change. I managed to get my front paws up, and then, with great effort, I got my chest on the counter. I scrambled feverishly with my back paws pumping, trying to wiggle my way on. Finally, one of my back paws caught onto a wooden nob, and I used that to push myself up.

At last, I stood on top of the counter with all the succulent food and the strange scratching noise. There was a giant piece of golden meat, bigger than anything I'd ever imagined, and my nose drew me to it. I started nibbling, but it was so big I couldn't get a good bite. I tried holding it down with one of my front paws while I tore at the legs of this giant animal, still warm from being taken from the box where Mom put food to get hot. Finally, using both paws to hold the meat in place, I managed to tear away several delicious pieces of the golden meat. But as I wrestled and groped, I didn't notice the large tray slowly moving across the countertop until it was too late. The tray wobbled on the edge before tumbling to the floor with a loud crash. I jumped back, startled, but fresh aromas set my nose twitching, bringing me back to the opportunities surrounding me.

I continued to explore all the delightful smells and tastes the countertop still offered. I found slices of rolled-up fish filled with other bits of fish and spicy bread. The fish was chewy, almost like the bouncy ball Jake and I played with. But unlike the ball, once I managed to tear off a shred of the fish, it tasted delicious. I gobbled up the tasty, chewy treat.

Next, I found a big white fish surrounded by vegetables on a tray, but a few nibbles were enough. The fish was too salty, and what dog likes vegetables? So I continued exploring for other delights. Some tasted sweeter than anything I'd ever eaten, but I sampled everything. One of the sweet treats stood very tall, with a delicious white covering on it, while others were no higher than the top of my paws, which made it easy for me to stand on them to hold them in place.

I buried my face in these wonderful sticky foods, soon covering myself in a mix of warm goo. I moved past the moist goodies to find more sweet pleasures. There were crunchy bars filled with nuts and a stack of flat goodies shaped like the saucers Jake had been teaching me to catch. These saucers were so thin they broke apart when I stepped on them, leaving a yummy coating of sweet white powder on my already gooey paws. I licked it off with delight.

Finally, I came to a tall pot. At last, the source of all the scratching noise I'd been hearing. It stood taller than me, and I couldn't see inside. So I again had to jump up on my back paws to explore. As I stood like a human, my front paws dangling over the front of the pot, the noise grew louder. I got my snout well inside and looked down to see what was causing all the noise. My eyes opened wide, and I yelped in surprise. Giant bugs scurried around in the large pot filled with water. I should have been frightened but was too fascinated to jump away. Oh, how I wish I had because what happened next made me look like a very bad boy.

Filled with curiosity, I watched while two giant bugs fought, climbing over each other in their frantic struggle to get out of the pot. Fascinated by the two wrestling bugs, I didn't notice the enormous claw from another beast slowly reach upward and, in a blur, latch onto my nose. I snorted in distress and desperately swung my head from side to side. But I couldn't get my attacker to release his painful grip. Panicked, I pulled away, knocking the entire pot onto its side, leaving the giant bugs to tumble out and fall to the floor, with me, dripping wet, right behind them.

I yelped again when I hit the ground, but at least I had broken from the painful grasp of that powerful claw. I barked at the giant bugs in my most authoritative big-boy bark, my fur straight up on my back, but they were so dumb they barely noticed. They scurried away while I, keeping a safe distance from their menacing claws, continued to bark madly, chasing them out of the room. Several times, the one who'd held my snout in his painful grasp turned to click his ugly claws at me. But with a final scary click, he turned away, leaving me to go back and eat all the fallen treats we'd knocked to the floor.

With my stomach full, I waddled over to a sunny spot by the window and curled up to doze in the warm sunlight. When I woke, the sun had moved, now sitting high in the sky. Where was my family? They'd been gone a long time. Then the sound of a car approaching. My tail thumped rapidly, and I peed in excitement, my anger and disappointment with them for leaving me alone all but forgotten. I was completely willing to put our little misunderstanding behind us.

I ran to the front door, stopping to grab one of the balls that had fallen from the tree to offer as a present for my long-missing family. I pranced with excitement, showing my prize, while I spun one way then the other. I expected they'd shower me with affection after such a long absence, but instead, they greeted me with shrieks and wailing. Then a quick rap on my bottom and shouts of "Bad, bad dog!" A large hand grabbed me and tossed me back in the small room, once again blocked off from the rest of the house but now by boxes stacked much higher than before.

With my tail between my legs and my ears flat against my head, I whimpered, unclear why everyone seemed upset. What had I done that made them so mad? I was in big trouble, and it was all so puzzling.

Confused and sad, I heard Mom's voice. "Where are the lobsters? Look at our turkey, my stuffed calamari, the bacala, my pies, the biscotti and pizzelli, and the lemon cake . . . all ruined! The only things he didn't get at were the fish dishes in the fridge I needed to prepare when we got back from the soup kitchen. John, please find those lobsters, and Jake, help me clean up this mess before the company starts arriving."

"Anna, please stay in the kitchen. Jake and I will be there in a minute to help. Just hold on."

If Mom sounded upset, Dad's voice burned with

anger, and my tail curled tighter between my legs.

"John, what's going on?"

"Mom, stay there. You don't wanna come in here just now."

Then more shrieks and Mom's voice again. "Oh no! Our tree! The quilt my mother made for Jake, torn to shreds!"

"Mom, it's okay, it's okay, we can fix it."

I heard Jake trying to console Mom, and my tail dropped even lower. I didn't know exactly why, but my little adventure had caused a lot of sadness, and I felt like *a very bad dog.*

"He didn't understand, Mom. He's just a puppy. I'll teach him. He'll learn. I'm really, really sorry." Jake kept repeating the same words over and over.

The room grew silent, and I heard Dad's voice again, now more sad than angry.

"I'm sorry, Jake. I don't know if this dog was a mistake. I know we promised you, but we need to know the family can volunteer at the shelter, go to church on Sundays, or head out to the movies and not come home to Armageddon. Your mother is just getting her strength back, and I won't do anything to risk your mother's health."

"John, you know you're not at your best when you're angry. Let's take a few minutes and pick up. I think we'll all feel better after we clean up this mess." Mom's voice was different now. It showed a strength I would hear a lot in the future when she wanted to make sure others listened. I'd learn Jake and Dad always fell silent when Mom used that voice.

The house grew quiet except for human footsteps

moving from room to room. At one point, Jake came to check on me, and my tail whipped, signaling my eagerness to play, but his eyes showed only sadness. He held me for a moment before putting me back down and returning to the others.

Finally, I heard Dad. "As usual, your mother was right, and I guess if nothing else this will be a Christmas Eve we won't soon forget. Good job rounding up the escaped lobsters, and I checked out the turkey. Minus a wing, but it'll be fine with a bit of triage. The puppy only ate two calamari. They're so chewy it probably slowed him down, and he barely touched the bacala. Doubtless, an acquired taste for dogs as well."

My tail wagged. Dad's voice stiff but no longer angry made me hope they might forgive me.

"Most of the deserts are recoverable. The cake is fine with some fresh frosting and a bit of reconstruction. So we're all set for the Feast of the Seven Fishes, just with fewer leftovers. Hon, I know you want to keep the traditions alive, but we have half the people we used to. Your folks are in Florida. My mom eats like a bird, and Frank's back in Iraq. Your brother will stop by because he loves your quohogs more than Karen's. But even Jake's ravenous crew won't empty our fridge, and the Fuentes won't have room in theirs for the food you'll send home with them."

Everyone fell silent as Dad grew calmer, like when he played with Jake in the backyard. But then his voice turned hard, and my tail stopped wagging.

"Now about the dog. You're both right, he's just a puppy, but we need to teach him because this *will not* happen again."

"Thanks, Dad."

"Don't thank me, champ. You're the one who will be teaching him, and you'll be held strictly accountable for his behavior. We'll help, but we told you when we got him, he's your responsibility.

"Now, about a name. We've been struggling the last few days, trying different names, and nothing seemed right. Based on today's evidence, I'd say this guy can do more damage than a bull in a china shop, and he's going to be as big as any dog I've seen. How about calling him Bull?"

"Bull . . . I like it. What do you think, Mom?"

"Well, it certainly fits. Now, can you both promise to keep Bull out of my kitchen while I get ready for our company? And Jake, it's probably a good idea to get Bull outside to play for a while. After the dietary adventure he just took, I expect he will have to take care of some business."

"Hum, yeah, good point, Mom. I'll get him out right now . . . and thanks again."

The tone in the other room slowly changed from anxious and angry to loving and happy. I couldn't figure out why, but it seemed to be because of this thing called Bull. So, after Jake came to take me out to play, I was delighted to discover I was Bull. Just like Jake, Dad, and Mom had a name, I now had one too.

Bull. It was my name, and it made me happy each time I heard one of them say it. My tail thumped with joy. They were talking about me.

Bull. It was my name in this family of ours.

Learning the Way

"I stopped off at the library last night on the way home from work. Lady there said this is one of the best for training puppies." Dad had that hard, demanding look in his eyes and handed Jake another one of those books he seemed to like so much. My Boy reached out to take it, his face shining bright, and dropped to the floor beside me. With elbows on the ground and his chin resting in his hands, Jake stared in fascination.

In the years to come, Jake had many books, lots with pictures of those metal birds that so captivated him, but this one was different. This book had pictures of dogs, and Jake looked at it like he wanted to remember every page. I sniffed the book and caught the faint scent of other dogs. Maybe that's what so interested Jake. Were these dogs coming to play with us?

"I've never been around dogs and don't know much about them. Training Bull is your responsibility. Is that understood?"

My ears perked as Dad mentioned my name. My tail swung high in the air while I jumped and ran around them, barking in excitement.

Mom laughed, and she reached out to turn Dad to face her. "*We* have our work cut out for us, but there's a very good boy inside Bull. He's smart as a whip. *We* just need to be patient and help Jake show him the way."

Mom's voice showed that strength again, and she stared directly at Dad. His eyes grew soft, and he leaned forward to kiss her.

"Yes, ma'am."

So, my journey to become not just a good boy but Jake's *Best Boy* began. Yes, my responsibilities to my family were clear, and the boy I loved was to show me the path to make them proud. I discovered tearing things up that weren't given to me to play with was not something his Best Boy would do. Neither was eating off the tables, but there was so much more to learn.

I spent the whole morning on the floor next to Jake while he switched between staring at the book and then playing games with me. Jake often stopped in the middle of a game to give me tasty little treats. Crazy humans, they'd forgotten to put food in my bowl that morning, but it was okay. I was happy just being with Jake, and we still managed to fill my morning hunger as we played together.

At first, the games seemed pretty silly and not as much fun as running around the backyard chasing a ball or wrestling with Jake. But slowly, I realized these were more than games. I'd follow a hand signal or a word from Jake to repeat the same action again and again.

"Sit."

"Stay."

"Come."

"Leave it."

Each time I followed his direction, Jake rewarded me with a treat and congratulations.

"Good job! Good boy!"

And sometimes my favorite: "My Best Boy."

I gobbled my latest treat and realized Jake was showing me how to make him, Mom, and Dad proud of me. No longer hungry, I still wanted to play. I wanted to learn everything I could to make them proud and to help make me their *Best Boy*.

Mom and Dad came into the room several times, smiling. Mom called me a *good boy* over and over while Dad watched closely with dark, discerning eyes and nodded with what I hoped was approval before leaving Jake to practice more with me.

"Okay, Jake, supper's on the table in a few minutes, but first, show us what Bull has learned today."

With Mom and Dad sitting on the couch, Jake and I showed them just how good a dog I could be.

I bet they were impressed watching me follow each of Jake's commands, even the really difficult ones. Once, Mom dropped a big slice of delicious-smelling warm meat right in front of me. My nose twitched with excitement. I was ready to pounce, but Jake's *leave it* command stopped me. I looked directly into his eyes, waiting until he nodded before swooping down to gobble it up. Then Jake opened the back door, shaking and squeaking my favorite chew toy, and threw it out into the small backyard. Excited, I took several giant bounds toward the door before Jake's voice rang out.

"Bull, stay."

I froze. My front paw raised and my tail pointing straight out behind me. All my instincts told me to chase that noisy furry toy. But Jake didn't want me to. So I lowered my paw, stopping at the door. I looked back as Jake and Mom clapped, shouting, "Good pup! Good dog! So smart! Who's my Best Boy?"

I turned to look at Dad, who had remained silent. He held my gaze a long time before nodding. Then, with his eyes growing softer, he reached down, picked me up in his powerful hands, and brought me close to his chest.

"I think you might just be one very special dog."

So, I'd started my journey in learning how to be not just a good dog but Jake's *Best Boy*. Dad put me down, and with my head held high, I trotted back to the arms of the boy I loved.

We played lots of similar games after that, and soon I had the *run of the whole house*. Even though I was getting big and could pull Jake anywhere I wanted, I'd learned not to jerk on the leash when we walked. I discovered the more attentive I stayed to Jake's signals, the more fun our walks became. I had endless freedom, allowed to linger and enjoy all the sights and smells surrounding me.

"Sorry, Bull, can't let you off-leash till we get to the park. It's silly cuz you're already so well-behaved, but Mom says it's not like the old days. The leash laws in town are super-strict. But, I promise, if no one's around, we'll get in a good run."

Dogs like to listen to their human's voices. If

they sound happy and confident, we are too. Of course, the words they say usually mean little to us, but I understood Jake. His bright smile told me I was a good boy.

I was happy simply being with Jake. I was especially excited and attentive this morning. We were walking toward the park. Soon we'd be away from the tight rows of houses with all their people and cars. Once away from all those distractions, Jake could take me off the leash, and I'd be able to run free. My head high and tail whipping wildly, I was tempted to pull Jake to get to the park quicker, but I didn't. I wanted to be his Best Boy.

My nose twitched, and I looked up to see Maria, the young girl who lived a few houses from my family, running to greet me. I liked Maria a lot, and she never missed us whenever we walked by. Her face lit with excitement. My friend dropped to her knees and hugged me, talking nonstop to Jake, of course, mostly about me. I heard her say my name a lot, but she also spoke to Jake about him and that school place where they spent so much time.

Unlike our home, Maria's house was packed with children. She had two small brothers who looked and sounded the same. But I had no problem telling them apart. Carlos greeted me first on each visit, with aggressive hugs and hard scratches on my chest, while José stood back, waiting for his brother to finish before coming forward to give me the most wonderful ear scratches. Her older brother Diego always came to greet me last. He was tall, almost as tall as Dad, but Diego moved slowly, like he'd been hurt. He didn't speak much, and when he did, he often repeated the same few words over and over.

The first time he saw me, I could smell Diego's fear, and I held back. But Jake smiled and signaled for me to lie down. Jake called the frightened boy over, took Diego's hand in his, and patiently showed the boy how to run his hands across my thick fur. Diego's trembling fingers moved across my back slowly, and his fear slipped away like a leaf floating to the ground. Jake let go, and Diego continued running his hand across my fur, giggling with pleasure. I'd made a new friend.

Diego was easily excited, so I learned to be careful, to move slowly around him, and not bark or do anything to startle him. In time, Diego wasn't frightened around me at all. Instead, he'd drop to his knees with his arms wide open as I raced over to say hello and have Diego swallow me up with his enthusiastic hugs.

I'd loved Jake from the moment he held me to his chest. But seeing how kindly and gently he treated Diego and how playful he was with Maria's younger brothers, I fell in love all over again.

After greeting me that day, Maria stepped aside and let the others say hello. When the younger brothers finished, she came to join me again, and I rested my head in her lap. With one final hug, Diego was gone. Giggling, he chased Jake, who ran across the yard, taking turns lifting the younger boys high into the air, carrying them on his shoulders. That goodness I saw in Jake the first day was there again for anyone to see as he played with the young brothers and the somehow-damaged older boy.

We played with Maria's family a long time this day, but I jumped up from some paw-thumping Diego belly rubs the moment Jake stirred. Like me, he was ready to get to the park.

"Mind if I join you?" Maria, her eyes bright with anticipation, watched Jake clip my leash back on.

He shrugged and handed the leash to Maria, and we walked out toward the street.

My tail swished with delight when Maria took my leash. She always paid so much attention to me, and her chest scratches were the best. Like Diego, she knew exactly what spots to scratch to set my back paw thumping with pleasure. Jake was nice to Maria, but he seemed preoccupied around her, like an older dog might be with a more energetic younger pup. I usually acted more excited to have Maria join us on our walk than Jake.

As we entered the park, I stopped to sniff a freshly marked spot and heard Maria's voice.

"Can't believe how big Bull's gotten. What's he weigh now?"

"About ninety-five pounds. The vet said he might hit one twenty."

"Wow, he was so small when we first saw him last Christmas Eve. I wish my papa would let me get a dog. But he says the house is too small, and the twins are too young to help. I don't mind the extra work, but he goes on about me doing normal kid stuff. And he's stressed with Diego getting older. I've given up. Guess I'll have to steal more time with Bull. Remember, call me any time you or your mom need help, walks, feeding him, anything she needs. How is she . . . your mom?"

"Better, I guess." Jake's voice sounded strange, like he didn't want to talk about something.

"Please say hi, and give her my regards."

"You're a funny one."

"Huh?" Maria stopped walking and turned to look at Jake

"Nothing, it's just how many twelve-year-old girls say, 'Give her my regards'?"

"I'll be thirteen next month, and what's age got to do with anything? Are you some kinda man of the world cuz you're fourteen? Your mother's a very special person, better than you deserve, and I wanted her to know I was thinking of her."

"All right, all right. Sorry, I didn't mean anything. Jeez, you get hot so easy."

As their voices grew louder, my ears dropped tight to my head, and I pulled my tail between my legs. Two of my most favorite humans were behaving so badly. They walked on in silence, my walk no longer so much fun. Finally, Jake unclipped my leash to let me roam and sat on a bench next to Maria as my friends stared at the ground, kicking the dirt at their feet.

Usually, they'd find a stick for me to chase, but today they both sat quiet and gloomy. Had they forgotten how to play? I jumped up, forcing them both off the bench. I ran from one to the other, holding my head low, rocking side to side, and I play-bowed in front of each of them. Then, I offered a low growl and jumped back up, challenging them to chase me. I growled one last time in my deepest big boy growl, waiting for a signal.

"All right, big guy, you're in for it," Maria called out, her anger, at least for the moment, forgotten.

Her words were followed quickly by Jake's laughing challenge. "Okay, Bull, we'll show who's the king of this here park."

I ran off to the park's far reaches, with shouts of joy and squeals of laughter in my trail. We ran and ran until exhausted, then fell in the tall grass high up on the hillside overlooking the park. My young friends lay next to each other, their shoulders almost touching, resting their heads against my panting chest and staring up at the sky. Whatever had made them so angry forgotten.

Then Maria began to speak again. "I was listening to some of my father's old albums, and I heard a song that kinda reminded me of the two of us. It's just a song, but the words are like poetry. It's called 'Dangling Conversations,' by Paul Simon. I liked the lyrics so much I wrote them down. Wanna read?"

Maria handed Jake something, and he rolled onto his stomach, resting his hands on his chin like he did when looking at those books he liked so much. Jake stared at the thing Maria gave him for some time before sitting up to look at her.

"Wow, that's beautiful. But how does it remind you of us? Yeah, we're probably the only two kids from the Flats who even read poetry, and I do like Robert Frost more than Emily Dickinson, but, I mean, it's like a *love* song. So I don't get the... "

"Ugh, Jake, you really are dense sometimes. The point isn't which poet you like. It's the fact you can't . . . We can't seem to . . ."

"Can't what? Aw, come on, Maria, don't get mad."

Maria jumped up and stormed away, her small hands tightly clenched by her side as she left Jake and me on the hillside, both of us puzzled by why our friend got so angry.

"I'll tell you, Bull, sometimes I don't get her. We can be hanging out, talkin' 'bout things I'd never talk with the guys about, and then, for reasons I can't figure, she just blows her top."

Watching Jake, I realized how easily humans could upset or misunderstand one another because of all the words they use. Why couldn't humans be more like dogs, enjoying the silence of being with the people they cared about? My young friends had so much to learn, and only time would tell if they'd learn those lessons.

I rubbed my body against Jake's leg, promising myself I would do all I could to help these humans I loved so much.

We walked past Maria's house on our way back from the park. I stopped by her gate and barked, calling for Maria, while Jake tugged impatiently on my leash, pulling my head forward. I kept looking at her house, but Jake, head down, marched away. I looked back one last time, but then my nose twitched toward our house.

Our pack was here!

I pulled on the leash to move him forward faster. My ears arched as our friends called out to us, and Jake released the leash, letting me gallop. My paws pounding across the pavement, I raced toward the two older boys who, along with my family and Maria's, had become the most important humans in my world.

Bikes clanged, falling to the ground, and a ball flew toward me. I caught it on the run and continued into our small front yard, met by the flashing feet and yells from the boys calling out while they chased me.

"Gimme that ball."

"You can run, but you can't hide."

The boys' names were Sam and Dougie, and we'd met the night of my little adventure with the giant bugs in our house. The boys came to our crowded home that night and immediately joined Jake on the floor while we all wrestled and played the *it's mine* game. One of my favorites. I'd played with my new friends all evening as the boys, watchful for grown-ups, slipped me treats.

They were filled with the energy and joy for the world around them all puppies and young boys seemed to have. But the two were different as can be. Sam was big, already taller than Dad, thickly built and powerful. Everything he did seemed deliberate and thought out. Calm, Sam moved slowly, the last to speak and with the least to say. But when he did talk, the others listened.

Unlike Sam, Dougie was a small ball of energy. He reminded me of Pepper the Jack Russell, who lived at the house where I was born. Dougie couldn't keep still, always moving, always talking, always laughing. I never followed what he was saying, but it didn't matter. It seemed to be the same for the humans around him. Dougie could chatter on with no one responding, everyone ignoring him like the people did while the noisy Pepper yapped non-stop. When someone barked at Dougie, telling him to be quiet, he'd giggle with glee. He'd gotten their attention. Dougie would stay silent a few moments before starting up chattering again while the others groaned or laughed because Dougie was off again, convinced everyone wanted to hear everything he had to say. I sometimes wondered if Dougie might have somehow come from the same litter as the stubby-tailed Pepper, but I was pretty sure that couldn't be.

Despite their differences, both boys cared for Jake just as he cared for them, and I accepted them into our pack. They always made time for me when they came to the house, throwing themselves onto the floor to wrestle and later slipping me treats under the table if they stayed to eat some of Mom's delicious food. Whether home or running with Jake around the park, the boys were often nearby, and we grew together, as did our bond of friendship.

My world had grown, thanks to My Boy and all his goodness. I found myself surrounded by more and more good people. But the center of that world for me, and I think for others, was the boy we all knew as Jake.

My World Grows

Darkness hung over the house, the morning light a hidden promise of things to come. I woke to the sound of Jake and Dad loading the car. I jumped up, barking to announce my pleasure, and circled them excitedly. Mom was up, handing them warm sandwiches with egg and cheese, which they gobbled while loading the car. I had to eat mine more slowly, patiently waiting while Mom broke off pieces, feeding me while the others worked.

Jake called me, and I hopped in the car. Mom came to the window to scratch under my chin. As we drove away, I smelled the agile cats who often sprawled on top of the sun-warmed stone wall that separated houses. I chased them the first time I saw them lying there so smugly, but my *leave it* game with Jake taught me to leave them alone. Then the yipping barks of the two small dogs who lived a few doors up from us filled the air, along with the distinctive early morning smells of food wafting through open windows and beneath doors of nearby houses. I sat with my head out the window, my ears and jowls flapping in the wind as the smells and sounds slowly faded.

I must have fallen asleep. When I woke, I looked out the window at a world I'd never known. Tall trees blocked the sun, and rotted leaves covered the ground leading to wide-open fields and streams. The scent of strange animals left my nose twitching and my tail thumping. I jumped from the car, trembling with pleasure. Tempted to run off, I quickly marked a nearby bush and turned back, my mouth open and panting.

Despite all the delights the strange new world had to offer, I stayed by Jake's side while he and Dad lifted packs onto their backs. We walked away from the tall trees to a hillside covered in high grass. Jake picked up a stick and looked at Dad, who nodded. Jake reached back and tossed the stick farther than I'd ever imagined, shouting: "Bring it!" My favorite game! But here in the wide-open space, it was so much more fun than in our small backyard or even the park near our house. Here, I flew over fallen trees and scurried under low branches, galloping on and on before finding the stick and picking it up softly in my mouth, running back to drop the prize by Jake's side. They continued walking through open fields and thick woods as I raced ahead, stopping to mark another bush, then barked in excitement for them to follow.

We stopped on one of the tallest hills, and Jake reached down to pick up a new stick. With a grunt, he threw it high over a cluster of trees. I lifted my eyes and watched it land in a big pool of water that I later heard Jake call a lake. I didn't hesitate. Bounding into the icy water seemed the most natural thing for me to do. I held my head high to spot the stick floating far off and paddled through the water until I reached my prize. I grabbed the stick in my mouth and swam back, bolting out of the water to drop it at Jake's feet. I shook with glee to get the water off my fur as Jake jumped back with high-pitched laughter.

We walked through the bright sunlight, and Jake continued throwing the stick in open fields or onto flat, cold stretches of water. I brushed against Jake's leg, relishing the newness of it all. For the rest of the day, I explored the amazingly different sounds and smells surrounding us. We were away from the noises of regular life, a place with sights and scents that called to me.

I'd never been here before, so why did it all feel so familiar?

At last we stopped to rest at the top of a rocky hill overlooking an open field. Jake gave me a cool drink of water, then Dad pushed big rocks together and, with darkness settling over our camp, built a glowing fire. Dad and Jake took one of the sacks from their back and drove long sticks into the ground, covering them with a big rough cloth. When they'd finished, it looked like a tiny house.

We ate, and the night turned cold. They added more wood to the fire and called me into the cloth house. I tried to curl up like I did at home to sleep for the night. But being inside, away from all the nearby smells and sounds, felt wrong. I sat up and whined. I couldn't lie still. Jake sensed my anxiousness and rubbed my chest, trying to calm me, but I continued to fidget.

Finally, Dad lifted the front flap to our little house, and I hurried to the opening. I turned around a few times before dropping to the ground, resting my head on my front paws, my nose outside our little house. With part of my body still brushing against Jake, I could now smell, see, and hear everything happening. After that night, I slept in this position whenever we camped. Most of my body would be inside our house, but my nose stayed poking outside.

My face warmed by the still bright flames of the fire, I sighed, contently on watch and remembering our day. The wonderful smell of the warm, fleshy fish they'd caught and cooked over the open fire lingered in the night air. Filled with pleasure and with Jake by my side, the glowing fire called to me. I yawned while the two men I loved talked long into the night.

"Good boy, you are a good boy. Did you see Bull jump in the water to retrieve the stick? It's like he's been doing it his whole life. It's unbelievable."

"It's terrific, Jake, but I think, in a way, he's been waiting thousands of years for you to throw that stick."

"What do you mean? Bull isn't even a year old."

"Hum, how to explain why he races into the water like that. All right, think of it this way."

My ears shifted as Dad's voice grew thoughtful.

"You know how humans and dogs have lived together for thousands of years? I think our relationship with Bull is truly a fantastic accomplishment."

Jake stopped scratching my chest. Something Dad said distracting him. "Accomplishment? Didn't it just happen?"

"It's more than luck. Imagine fifteen thousand years ago. No cities or towns. Humans don't know how to farm, plant crops, anything. They survive by hunting, fishing, gathering fruits and vegetables growing in the wild. Life's hard for these hunter-gatherers and for the wolves who hunt near them. Then something amazing happens. Humans and wolves discover they can work together. This new relationship makes both their lives easier."

"Sure, Dad, everyone knows dogs evolved from wolves, but I don't see how a wild, rabbit-eating wolf became a dog. It's hard to imagine how we got from a wild wolf to Bull contentedly lying here by my side."

Dad leaned forward to close the opening to our house a little more as the night air grew cooler.

"Since we got Bull, I started asking myself the same question. I've been reading some books from the library. It's incredible, and no one knows for sure how it all happened. Darwin, anthropologists, and historians can offer a glimpse, but no one can be certain."

"What do you think?"

"Well, I try to imagine a band of hunters searching for food. Over the centuries, they'd learned how to hunt for large animals, like elk or bison. Hunters discovered following wolves could lead them to the large herds, and wolves found when men attacked a herd, the wolves could separate a weaker animal from the pack. Wolves also learned that if they followed humans, they could feed on any remains left behind."

Dad smiled and paused a moment. "It's easy to envision the braver and smarter wolves trailing closer and closer to the humans. The wolves' howls at night warned humans of impending attacks, while the wolves, realizing predators would be scared away by the humans, crept ever closer to their bright fire. As the most curious wolves came closer, their howls warning of nearby predators made them welcome by the watchful humans tending the flames.

"Who knows how long it took. But the relationship grew. A grateful human tosses scraps to an attentive wolf, and the animals' comfort with humans increases. At some point, humans found a pup separated from its mother. The pup, struggling for survival, was ready to take that giant step toward the creation of the dog. Fed by humans and with no pack of its own, the wolf pup joined the humans in their nomadic life. That wolf pup had pups of her own, and being puppies, they instinctively showed love and tried to please the pack member who looked after them. As they worked to please their humans, their new pack grew to value and love them back."

"Gee, Dad, you almost sound like a romantic."

"I guess I do." Dad's voice grew soft and thoughtful. "Bull's changed me, made me see things differently. The books describe how dogs learned to help, and as humans developed new skills, the dogs did too. Dogs learned to herd and protect livestock from predators while performing hundreds of other tasks. Humans trained dogs to quietly walk in the woods and hold still while pointing to the game the hunter searched for. Frozen, motionless, the dog waited for a command, then bounded into the water and grabbed the animal with a soft mouth. They'd carry the prey back and drop it at their hunting partner's feet and wait for a new command."

Jake's petting slowed, and he turned to look at Dad. "So when Bull jumped into the water, grabbed the stick, and carried it back to me, it was something his ancestors have done for thousands of years?"

"That's what the books say. I've thought a lot about Bull. Studied him, kinda." Dad leaned forward and joined Jake in petting me. "Bull's no purebred, but you can see a lot of retriever in him. He's smart as a whip, loves the water, and loves to please and be with people. Look at his webbed toes. Perfect for swimming. Based on his size, plus the thickness of his coat, I'm guessing he's part Newfoundland as well. I read Newfies are consummate water dogs. Fishermen trained them to help drag in their giant nets, and today they still work, saving swimmers in danger of drowning. When Lewis and Clark journeyed across America, they had a Newfoundland named Seaman with them. I saw some terrific books about Seaman's contributions on the journey. I noticed your to-read book pile is getting low. We can pick up a few when we swing by the library.

"Bull's a great dog. There's something rare and special in him, but this bond is no accident. You can call it fate, but Bull is the product of thousands of years of love between humans and dogs. His actions appear amazing, but ancient memories lie deep within him. He's the perfect example of selfless love. The domestication of dogs is one of society's greatest accomplishments, but maybe dogs deserve the credit. Imagine if humans could do the same with our own diverse cultures, loving each other and placing the needs of the other ahead of ourselves. I might be naïve, but I believe in man's ability to become better. And dogs might just be the ones to show us the way."

Jake turned his attention back to me and scratched under my chin. "Wow, Dad, all those life lessons in this giant fur ball at my feet?"

"I got a little preachy, but please indulge your old man a minute more. Life is a precious gift. We should leave the world better than we found it. Sadly, dogs often do a better job than humans. Bull has a lot to teach us if we pay attention."

"I think you're right, Dad, about fate, I mean. When I started training Bull, I read about how a dog often picks the human, and not the other way around. I remember the day we went to get a puppy. It's weird, but from the minute we walked into that room and approached the box, I saw Bull looking right at me. It's like there were no other puppies there. Like he knew he was the one for me. Like he knew something none of the rest of us did."

I lay curled next to Jake as he scratched behind my ears. He and Dad were talking about me. I heard them say *dogs* and my name, but I felt like what they talked about was bigger and more important than just me. I sighed contentedly, lowered my head onto my paws, and thought back to Jake picking me up that first day. I remember it felt like I had known him since before I was born. Now, while Dad talked, it seemed like he was explaining how that feeling was possible.

I didn't need to understand all of their words. I didn't need anything more than just being with Jake and Dad. I was doing my job loving, protecting, and making them proud. I'd leave it to Jake to understand those other bits, and I was glad Dad was there to teach him.

Looking out into the fire, my eyes blinked, staying closed longer each time until I fell asleep, my body resting lightly against Jake's. The sounds of my humans' voices slipped away, and the world around me slowly changed.

Since I was a young pup, I often had images of other moments that came to me when sleeping deeply. Sometimes these moments felt like nothing more than memories of things that might have happened or perhaps could happen: playing with Jake or just running in the sunshine. When I'd wake, I didn't dwell on the images. The real moments of life kept me busy enough. Even when the image frightened me, I might open my eyes and *welp* or grunt, only to feel Jake's gentle touch. I'd hear his reassuring voice, "It's all right, Bull, you were only dreaming.", and I'd be at ease, the images all but forgotten.

But what happened that night was different, and though the memory stayed with me all these years, I've never been able to entirely understand it. I remember falling asleep next to Jake, and then, I wasn't sleeping.

I'm lying in an open area surrounded by tall

trees, staring into the flames of a much larger fire where several families gather, drawing warmth from the bright blaze. My belly is full of freshly cooked meat, and I contentedly chew on a giant fresh bone while a boy younger than Jake curls up next to me. He has one arm draped over my shoulder as he sleeps, his body moving gently with each breath. I stare into the flickering fire. I won't sleep. I have a job to do. I will stay awake through the night, alert for danger, waiting until the others in my pack begin to stir with the morning light. Only then, ever so briefly, while my pack collects their things, do I sleep. Soon they strap a sack onto my back with a rope, and we are off again, searching for our next meal.

When we leave camp, the boy is free to wander from the trail, but I'm always by his side. He picks up a stick to play with, and he runs toward a dark cluster of trees. The boy plays hunting games, copying the actions of the older men, but he's strayed too far. I bark my deep warning bark, and I run after him as he continues to roam farther from our pack. I see a woman with a smaller child resting on her hip. The woman takes several steps toward us and lovingly shouts to the boy in words I don't understand. The boy stops and, laughing, runs back to catch up with the pack while I gallop just behind, ever watchful. Off in the distance, leading the pack, a man, broad-shouldered and powerful, stands on a hillside. He is holding a long, sharp stick. The man stops to look back, checking to see where the boy and woman are. Our eyes meet. I know those eyes. I have stared into those hard eyes before. He holds my gaze until the boy and woman get closer. Then he nods to me with a knowing look, and he turns back to lead our family in search of our next meal.

I woke to Jake's touch, a cool night air rustling my fur. Jake stirred as he curled closer to me inside our cloth house. I closed my eyes, but sleep wouldn't come, and I tried to understand what happened. It all felt so real, so natural, me sitting by the giant fire with my pack. Later, the sack tied to my back, I carried supplies for my family. The boy, so much like Jake, the woman, and the man . . . That man.

I'd think about that night with Dad and Jake by my side often as time passed. I'd think of Dad telling his story, with me staring into the glow of the bright fire of another time and place that I never entirely understood. Yes, all these memories connecting me to something primal and ancient left me happy. I felt like they were all pieces of what I was for Jake, and he for me.

Now, so many years later, with my old bones sore and achy, I find myself thinking more and more of that night. I see myself, young and strong again, running alongside the boy who reminds me so much of Jake, protecting him from unseen dangers.

PART II

Changing Seasons

Things were changing. A cool breeze blew across my face, and I hadn't dug a hole in our yard to escape the heat in days. My fur was getting thick again. It wouldn't be long before I wouldn't get to spend the whole day with Jake.

"Come on, get your nose out of that book." Dougie reached down to grab the book from Jake's hand. "I don't get it. Any information you could possibly want is a computer click away. Movies, news, it's all there for you. YouTube and Twitter tellin' you everythin' that's happenin' in the world. And if you actually care about what some old dead guys thought, that info is a click away too. More important stuff is happenin' out there. We are days away from our first day of *high school*, and we have to be ready."

Jake looked up from his bed and smiled while Dougie held the book behind his back. "Ready for exactly what, Dougie?"

"Ready for what? Ready for *the girls* in high school. So no more books! Come on. We only have a few more days of summer. You're in your bedroom wastin' time readin' books and writin' those stories of yours. Look at your desk. Fitzgerald, Hemingway, Hesse, what is this stuff? Dude, we gotta go. I saw my cousin with some of her friends at the park playin' Frisbee. I told her we'd come right back and hang out. I can't just take Sam, here. He hasn't spoken to a girl since first grade when he told Tina Ferzoco to stop followin' him during recess. With a wingman like that, what kind of a chance do I have with high school girls?"

"All right, I'll come, but just for clarification, these high school girls you are so excited about. You do realize they were all in eighth grade with us just a few months ago?" Jake shook his head as he spoke and grew silent again. He could tell Dougie had a lot more to say.

"All true, Jake, my boy, but they've had an entire summer to grow up, and man, how some of them have grown. Now they are days away from officially bein' high school girls. A world of difference. A world of difference. Come on, let's take Bull. Girls like him better than any of us, and they find his silence charmin' where Sam's is downright annoyin'."

"There is nothing annoying about me."

My ears perked at the sound of Sam's powerful voice.

"Wrong again, *Sammy Alphabet*. Your silence is annoyin', and some, Tina Ferzoco among them, might say downright scary."

"Don't call me that. I told you I don't like it." Sam's voice grew even louder.

Dougie continued running around the room, yipping and yapping like the Jack Russell he reminded me so much of, while Jake rested on his bed, reaching for another book. Sam usually stayed quiet, but just like with a big dog, it was wise not to push him too far. Jake raised his head from his new book, grinning, while Dougie continued to yip away, unaware of the change in Sam.

"Well, it beats the hell out of Sam Szczepanski! Do you remember, Jake? First grade, Sister Francis De Sale's? She asks Sam how to pronounce his name, and he proceeds to deliver the longest speech in his entire elementary school career. Our man Sam stands up with a stone-cold look on his face, says 'It's pronounced just how it's spelled. Szczepanski. S, Z, C, Z, E, P, A, N, S, K, I, Szczepanski.' Then he plops back down at his desk, folds his arms and smiles for the only time all year, fully content with his performance. *Sammy Alphabet* was born that day and will live on in the annals of Sacred Heart Elementary School."

Sam reached out, grabbing the smaller boy and locking his powerful arms around Dougie's head. Dougie yelped, but it was like a pup pretending to be hurt. Smiling, he continued to chatter away as Sam allowed him to slip from his grasp.

"All right, no more Sammy Alphabet. Mister Szczepanski *pronounced just how it's spelled.* But whatever we call you, Mister S, you're gonna have to learn sooner or later not to tell girls *to stop followin' you around* and actually have somethin' to say to them. So come on, let's go. Somethin' tells me you might need a lot of practice at this."

With a whoop of excitement, Dougie came over,

clipping my leash on as he continued yapping in the way only Dougie could. I felt his joy for life and the same energy bubbling over from the other boys as we flew from the house. We ran down the street. All of us young and full of wonder for the world around us, racing toward just what none of us quite seemed to know.

Stories From the Past

"Mom seems better."

"Yes, I think Bull has helped a lot bringing her back to us."

We were hiking from our campsite back to the spot where Mom dropped us off in the car several days earlier, and my ears perked at Dad's mention of my name.

"You are old enough now. I want to share some things. This last miscarriage hit your mother particularly hard. She has so much love to give and was so excited this time when it looked like we'd made it through the danger zone. The last sonogram showed it was a girl, and it still hurts your mother to think about the girl we hoped to bring into our family.

"Jake, I know your mom and I can be overprotective at times, but you have to realize, in a way, you truly are a miracle. You know you were ten weeks premature. You weren't supposed to make it. After you were born, your mother spent three straight weeks at the hospital. She refused to leave your side. Your mother is one determined woman.

She all but forced them to rewrite the rulebook in the prenatal intensive care unit. She immersed herself in ensuring you got the best care possible. The staff at the hospital were terrific, but your mother didn't let the slightest detail go unaddressed. She didn't worry about hurting feelings, made sure she understood every aspect of your care, and wasn't afraid to challenge anything that fell short of what she felt was best for you. I never saw five feet two inches stand so tall.

"She was an absolute lioness, strong, fearless, and oh so charming when she had to be. Watching her look after you in that hospital, I think I fell in love with her all over again."

"Gee, Dad, I knew I was premature, but Mom never talked about how serious it all was."

"It's all true, and that's why this last miscarriage hit your mother so hard. I saw that look in her eyes again. She'd geared up for battle one last time and was going to do whatever she had to for this baby. She quit work, stayed home, followed all the doctor's orders, and it looked like we'd made it. But then, with no warning, she started bleeding, and . . . well, you know the rest.

"I never saw your mom so beaten. Her vitality and strength abandoned her. She was in a malaise that nothing seemed to help. I was scared, but as if God knew we needed help, this Bull in a china shop came into our lives. I still see sadness, sometimes, hidden behind your mother's bright eyes. It's something she'll carry a long time. It may follow her the rest of her life. I think the pain of losing a child is something that never fully leaves you. But when I look at her laughing, watching you play with Bull, I see that passion for life coming back into your mother's wonderful heart."

We walked toward the car, and I brushed against Jake's side as his gentle young hand ruffled my ears. I listened to the wonderful sound of Dad's voice, so strong and reassuring. Hearing my name and Mom's, I knew somehow, even far away from her, I was helping her and this family.

"Thanks for telling me all this, Dad. Most of my friend's parents don't talk to them . . . at least not about things like this."

"You deserve nothing less, Jake. Life isn't easy, and your mother and I may not always be there for you. And even if we are blessed to be, we can't, we won't, live your life for you. Life isn't fair, and the only thing you ultimately can control is how you handle the good fortune and hardships that come your way. The courage your mother's shown is an inspiration to me. She's a strong woman, much stronger than I am. She stood by me when I pulled myself out of a very dark place, but that's a story for another time.

"I'd be wrong not to share your mother's story because it's a part of who you are. She's an amazing woman, and we are lucky to have her."

Jake stopped to fix the pack on his back, pausing a long time before he turned to look at Dad. "Can I ask you something? The dark place . . . Vietnam. Why don't you ever talk about it?"

"Oof . . . okay. I'd hoped you'd be a bit older, but maybe it's time."

Dad's voice was strained, lacking its usual confident tone. Instead, he sounded frightened, but Dad wasn't afraid of anything. My tail drooped as the man I knew so well grew somehow smaller.

"Jake, I wasn't a perfect kid. I had a terrible temper. I ran with a rough crowd and made mistakes. During my senior year in high school, I got in a fight and hurt another kid . . . badly. The kid was a bit of a jerk, but he didn't deserve what I did to him after I got him on the ground. I should've walked away, but I kept hitting him. Wouldn't stop. It took three teachers to pull me off. He ended up in the hospital with a broken jaw and a detached retina. Lucky I didn't blind him. If he was a kid from the Flats or another working-class neighborhood, I probably could've gotten away with it, but he came from the Hill, his old man was some kind of judge. They brought me up on some serious charges, and it seemed the easiest way to make it all go away was to enlist.

"Vietnam was in the news every day back then. Body count, protesters. None of us knew what to make of it all, but no one in my world was protesting or going to Canada. It's a story as old as war itself. The poor kids end up on the front lines, while the children of the rich or powerful are kept safe. So I joined the Army and within a few months was crawling through rice paddies in Vietnam."

"Was it as bad as people say?"

"Well . . . yes and no. I saw some of the best and worst of humanity."

Dad stopped walking, and he signaled for Jake to sit on a large rock that looked back at the long trail we'd hiked. Dad sat next to him, sighed, squinted into the late-afternoon sun, and began to talk again.

"By the time I got to Vietnam, the war was being fought in sound bites on the evening news. The Tet Offensive, Mỹ Lai, Kent State were all in the rearview mirror. Politicians were looking to keep votes and find the easiest way out of a seemingly bottomless pit. By then, most of the guys in Vietnam had been drafted and didn't want to be there. For me, it was a twelve-month tour of Russian roulette. Keep your head down, have your buddy's back like he has yours, and try to get home in one piece.

"War is ugly, real ugly. And knowing you've taken another person's life is something you carry with you forever. It changes you in ways words can't capture. But bad as it could get over there, being back home was worse. Over there, we'd count the days of our tour, telling ourselves everything would be fine once we got back home. But none of us had a clue what was waiting for us."

Dad reached down and picked up a rock. He stared at it for the longest time, shifting it from one hand to the other. I stood, excited, thinking he would throw it. I hoped if we played our *bring it* game, it might pull Dad out of his sadness and make him talk about something happy. I barked, signaling Dad to play, but he didn't notice. Instead, he dropped the rock at his feet and, with his voice sadder than I'd ever heard, continued talking.

"It's 1973. I'm at Logan Airport, still in uniform, waiting at a carousel for my duffle bag. I see two really cute girls, blonde hair, blue eyes, wearing faded cut-off jeans and these tie-dyed shirts that were in style, and I think to myself, I'm home. One of the girls is staring at me, and I smile. She walks over, stops in front of me, spits on the ground, and says, *You should be ashamed of yourself.*"

"What an ugly thing to say."

The anger in Jake's voice frightened me. I didn't understand what Dad was talking about, but it upset both of them, and I wanted to help. I walked over to Dad and brushed my side against his leg. He scratched behind my ears and took a deep breath, a sad smile appearing for a moment before getting lost in his painful memories. I nuzzled under his hands, hoping to distract him and get more pets, but he had more to say. I sighed. There was nothing I could do, so I rested my head in Dad's lap as he continued.

"They didn't know any better. Years ago, I heard someone say everyone who came back from Vietnam came home alone. That sure was true for me, and I remained alone for a long time. I don't think I felt home again until I met your mom. It took a long time before I had a good night's sleep, and I still have bad nights. But having your mother and you in my life has made all the difference."

Dad's voice changed, and he stood up, starting to walk again. My tail curled beneath me, sensing his pain. Listening to his father seemed to fill Jake with sadness too. Anxiously, I watched them walk side by side, father and son, their shoulders straight. Dad began to speak again.

"*Welcome home, son.* You heard it from the well-meaning old-timers in the barbershops and barrooms. People wanted to know every painful detail of what happened over there, or they were calling you a 'baby killer.' The next few years weren't good ones for me. There were a lot of drugs in Vietnam, and I continued playing with some dangerous stuff once I got back. I kept myself numb between the drugs and alcohol from one day to the next until finally . . . I met your mother.

"I'm almost ten years older than her, but she's wiser than me in so many ways. I knew she was special the moment I met her, and I think she saw something in me. She told me she had a vision for her life, and spending it with an angry drunk wasn't part of it. I walked into my first AA meeting the next day and haven't had a drink in more than twenty years.

"I'm not saying I wouldn't have found my way out of those dark times without your mother. Ultimately, whatever we do in life, good or bad, is on us. But God knows your mother made my journey a better one. I hope someday you find someone as decent and loving as I did."

I saw Mom leaning against the car, waiting for us, and I barked, racing ahead to greet her. I tried not to, but I couldn't resist. I jumped up on my back paws. I was almost as tall as Mom now when I stood up like that, so it was easy for me to smother her with kisses. I was prepared to stop if Mom or Jake told me to get down, but no one did, so I reveled in my indulgence, showing Mom how much I loved her. Mom looked stronger now, better every day. She laughed often, and her touch, although still gentle, had strength and vitality that wasn't there in those early days when I'd rest in her lap while she wept.

Dad smiled patiently, waiting as I showed Mom how much I cared. Then he nudged me aside with his hip and picked Mom up from the waist, spinning her around as she laughed and kissed him. Putting her down, Dad held her face gently in his hands and looked into her eyes. Dogs can tell a lot about what humans think or feel by looking into their eyes, but most humans lack that ability. Mom and Dad were not like most humans.

On the drive, I didn't sit with my nose out the window with the wind blowing in my face like I usually did. Instead, I rested my head in Jake's lap, listening to my family's voices while they sang, talked, and laughed all the long ride home.

New Ball Game

Mom no longer stayed home all day, and I was left alone for long periods. But Jake always got up early to take me for a walk around the neighborhood. When we left the house, I could tell by Jake's mood and the pace we walked if it would be long or just for me to do my business.

Most morning walks were short, with no stops to visit Maria and her brothers or time to play with the older boys at the park. Sometimes on our walks, Jake brought a ball to throw and let me chase it around the park until I was gasping for breath, but if someone we didn't know came along, he'd call me to sit by his side until the stranger walked on. I didn't like this *stay* game much, but I loved being with Jake and trusted him. It didn't matter what we did because we were together.

When the boys played their games, Jake brought my long leash and tied it to the bench next to the field, leaving me with a bowl of cool water. On warm days, I'd dig a hole and lie under the bench to watch Jake play. He often ran over to pet me or check my water. But mostly, he ran, waving his stick or chasing and kicking a ball.

Some of the boys were bigger than Jake, but no one ran faster. Jake was never far from the ball. It seemed like he knew, before the others, which way the ball would go.

Often, Maria showed up. She'd untie me and bring me up with her brothers to sit on the hillside under the shade of the tall trees, watching the boys play in the field below. Her brothers would shout and clap as Jake flashed across the grass, faster, stronger, happier than the others who raced after him. Maria didn't cheer or yell like her brothers, but her eyes never left Jake wherever he went on the field. She looked at Jake the same way Mom and Dad looked at each other. Maria saw how special Jake could be, and my love for her grew stronger.

But this day as we left the house, Jake moved mindlessly. He let me linger, marking every tree, shrub, or post we passed. He was in no hurry, and I relished the relaxed walk with My Boy.

My nose twitched with excitement. A new dog had moved nearby. I'd heard the calls in the night, and now I found her scent as I marked another tree. I decided I'd have to sneak through that hole under our fence and introduce myself one of these nights.

But not today. This was my special time with Jake. My family called the mornings Jake didn't rush our walks *weekends,* and this morning must be one because Jake trailed behind me, kicking a rock down the path while he talked.

"I met a girl, Bull. I like her. A lot. And I think she likes me, but I can't tell for sure. I don't even know how to talk to her. The only one I'm good at talking to is you, and that's because you're such a great listener.

"High school's so much different than junior high. The kids are from all across town. Some come from real wealthy families, and almost all the juniors and seniors have cars. Sometimes I feel like such a goof riding my bike there. I see how the kids from the Hill snicker when they see me eating the lunch I bring from home instead of buying the cafeteria food. It's a good thing Sam and Dougie are there, but it's still hard. And when it comes to talking about girls? Forget it. I could never trust Dougie. The whole town would know my secrets. And Sam . . . well, you know Sam. I can't get three words out of him."

Jake's voice grew more serious the longer he spoke. I stopped to look up at him, and he reached down to run his hand across my flank.

"Which, my friend, is why you get to hear all this. So, here's the story. The other day, I saw Skyler. That's her name: Skyler. I always thought it was a kinda weird name, but now I just feel anxious and excited whenever I hear it. Well, anyway, the other day, I'm on my bike coming down from the Hill after cutting a few lawns, and I stopped at a light by the country club. A flashy convertible pulls up next to me with a bunch of older kids eating McDonald's, laughing, a couple of them throwing wrappers onto the street.

"I recognized the driver, Kyle Vandenberg. He's a junior, and his father's a big-shot real estate developer converting one of the abandoned mills along the river into condominiums. Kyle looks at me and asks what horsepower my bike has. He makes like he's going to offer me a fry, then pulls his hand back and drives off across the intersection moments before the light changed to green. It's weird. Even though Skyler laughed, she seemed kinda embarrassed, like she knew Kyle was acting like a jerk.

"Anyway, I'm up early the next day. I'd signed up for spring chorus, so I went to the auditorium before first period for tryouts, and Skyler was there. That's how I learned her name. Kind of pretty, huh? The name, not her, but jeez, she is pretty, really pretty. Blonde with beautiful blue eyes. But it's more than that. She just seems different. Stylish, in control, not anything like the other girls I've known.

"I think she smiled at me when we went around and introduced ourselves. I don't know if she recognized me from the other day, but I think she might have. Now I wanna talk to her, but I don't know what to say. I hate to admit it, but I'm flat-out scared. I know what Mom or Dad would say. Any girl would be lucky, blah, blah, blah."

We stopped, and Jake sat on the bench where I watched him play his games. He continued to talk, his hand gently resting on my back. He had grown. Much taller than Mom now, Jake's voice had gotten deeper, but it still had the kindest tone whenever he spoke to me. Usually, Jake talked about things like what a good boy I was, how smart I was, or he'd tell me the rules of whatever game we were going to play and what I had to do to make him proud.

"Be patient with Diego."

"Don't chase that cat."

"Don't pee on this lawn because the people who live there get mad."

I relaxed around Jake because I knew he had things under control, but this felt different. Jake was struggling to find answers, and I didn't know if I could help. He'd mentioned Mom and Dad, so I thought they might come and join us on our long walk like they sometimes did. But he also kept saying the word Skyler. I didn't know it yet, but Skyler was to play a big part in our story.

Jake's words were confusing, but he needed me to be there for him, so I put my head in his lap as he sat on the bench, staring off into the distance. He leaned forward to scratch my chest, and my tail swung across the ground, raising dust around us. Jake jumped back, laughing. I was somehow helping.

Jake started again, his voice different, like whenever he was proud of me for learning a new trick. This time, though, it wasn't me who had learned something. Instead, I think Jake had. Now he sounded very pleased with himself.

"It's funny, whenever I'm afraid to do anything, Dad tells me, 'Sometimes you have to take that long walk across the gym floor and ask the girl to dance.' I never really understood what he meant, but it makes sense now. I guess it doesn't matter what I say. I just have to be willing to say something. I'll never know unless I try. That's it, Bull. I'm just going to talk to her next time I see her. I'm gonna tell her she has a nice voice and ask her if she likes dogs. It's a deal killer if she doesn't like dogs."

Jake laughed, acting very pleased with himself as

he locked one of his arms around my neck and pulled me to the ground with joyful aggression. He wanted to wrestle, and I loved to play rough like this. When Mom was around, she'd nervously scold us, telling Jake he played too rough and we might hurt each other or break a piece of furniture. But seeing how much we enjoyed ourselves, she'd sigh and smile, letting us play on. Of course, I always made sure I used my soft mouth when we wrestled and rolled on the ground, pulling on his arm or leg, but if we were out of Mom's sight, our play had fewer rules.

That day, with no grown-up near, we wrestled longer and harder than we ever had. Boundless energy filled us, and it needed to be released. Whatever worries Jake had floated away like fluffy white clouds racing across the sky on a windy spring day as we rolled around and around on the ground in the dusty park.

Jake was happy, and I'd helped. He'd found something he was looking for, but only time would tell if the thing Jake found was what he needed most.

Skyler

Now I understood, Skyler wasn't just a word, it was a name. A girl's name. A girl who meant a lot to Jake.

She came to the house for dinner, and Jake couldn't stop looking at her. Skyler squealed when she first saw me and dropped to the ground to pet me. She said what a good-looking boy I was, but she didn't really seem interested. If I were younger, I might have taken offense, but Jake appeared a little less interested in me when Skyler was around as well. So I didn't judge too harshly if Skyler acted preoccupied with Jake. I thought about how some dogs can forget about their humans when other dogs are around. I could understand Jake getting a bit inattentive when Skyler was nearby, and wow, she was around a lot. And when Jake wasn't home, he was either at school or with Skyler. I'd hear Mom and Dad saying their names together a lot, as if, just like me, they were wondering where he'd gone. Then, when Jake did come home, I could smell Skyler on his clothes.

Mom and Dad had taken me out for a walk. It

had been one of those days when my family didn't leave me, but Jake went out early that morning and hadn't returned. The sky was growing dark, and I listened to Mom and Dad as they kept mentioning his name, making me miss Jake more and more.

"I don't know, Anna. I understand Jake's crazy about her, and he's not a frivolous kid, but something is missing with the girl. A lack of, ah, I don't know. Something."

"You've always had almost unreasonably high standards, John. Admittedly, even more for yourself than others. But are you sure you're fair about her? Maybe you're a little jealous Jake doesn't have the time for you he used to?"

"You don't believe that?"

"Sorry, no, I don't. Well, maybe a little. It's just I know we all miss having Jake underfoot. I think Bull most of all. But as you say, Jake is crazy about her. I just keep reminding myself he's an incredibly grounded young man. When the time comes, Jake will find a partner who will be everything he deserves. Maybe Skyler's the one, and maybe she isn't, but if we want to keep our son in our lives, we better be sure whoever he ends up with is someone we open our hearts to."

We arrived back at our house, and they sat on the front steps while I curled up on the walk at their feet. No one said it, but I think everyone was waiting to see if Jake would be home soon. Dad reached down to scratch under my chin.

"You're right. I married a wise woman, and maybe that's the problem. I'm trying to compare Skyler to you, and anyone would pale in comparison. I don't know. Maybe it's because her family's wealthy or her parents are separated and neither very involved in the girl's life. I just hope she has what it takes to stick through the good and bad times. God knows how many times I needed your strength. I want the same for Jake."

Mom gave Dad a small kiss, her eyes wet. "Trust your son. We've taught him well, and even in the throes of first love, he's wiser than you think. If Skyler is the one, Jake will see it, and if she isn't, I'm confident he'll figure that out as well."

"I'd just hate to see him make a foolish mistake."

My nose twitched, and I looked up to see Jake walking toward our house, holding Skyler's hand. Dad unclipped my leash, and I ran to Jake. I circled, barking, and Jake rewarded me with rough hugs before we hurried back to Mom and Dad. Jake dropped to the ground and wrestled with me while he spoke.

"Sorry, I should've called. We were out on Skyler's sailboat all day, and now we're starving. When we got back to her house, there wasn't a thing to eat, and I knew Mom wouldn't let us down."

"Come on. I've got ziti and eggplant parm I can warm up. But please call if you're going to miss supper." Mom pointed her finger at Jake. She tried to scold Jake for making us miss him so much, but she couldn't hide her smile and how pleased she was to have him back.

Then Dad called out, "Come on in, Skyler. Our house is your house."

I walked back to brush against Skyler to show her she was welcome, but she hesitated, her eyes looking at everything and no one. So, I continued to brush along Skyler's leg, my tail wagging as we followed my happy family into the house, but she never reached down to touch me.

"Oh my, everything smells wonderful, and Bull is such a good dog."

Skyler said my name, but still, she didn't touch me. Confused, I left her side and entered the house, searching for My Boy.

Yes I Can

Jake was taller than Dad now, but he'd changed in other ways too. Not only taller, his body was also different. He used to move all gangly and loose, like a pup that hadn't finished growing. But Jake's body had grown thicker and more powerful.

When he played his game with the stick chasing the small ball, he still raced across the field faster than the other boys. And, like before, he still somehow knew where the ball would be before the others did. But now, he bounced off the other boys as they collided, often leaving others sprawled on the ground. When he was younger, Jake avoided the other players while he raced with the ball, darting in and out. Now he'd seek out the collision, knowing his body wouldn't betray him.

As young and strong as we were that warm, sunny day, it was hard to believe either of our bodies would ever be tested, but challenges lay ahead that neither of us could have imagined.

After another of their games, we lay on the hillside overlooking the field while the boys talked. Or, more accurately, Jake and Sam listened to

Dougie yipping on and on.

"I'm tellin' ya for the last time, I don't know what's up with you two and all the college prep classes you're takin'. We're barely halfway through high school, and the boredom is killin' me. There is no way I'm signin' on for four more years of lectures and books."

Jake smiled, staring into the clear sky like he was searching for one of those giant birds he watched so often.

"Don't give me that smirk, DiSpirito. I know that look. You got those stars in your eyes again."

"Sorry, Dougie, I've got dreams. Flying jets is part of that dream, and they won't let you do that with just a high school diploma."

"Mister *I got a dream*. Whaddya think you're too good for this town? Okay, say you go off to the Air Force Academy, get some fancy degree, and learn to fly. I'm tellin' ya, you belong here. This is where the people who care about you are. This is home. At least Sammy's plan makes some sense. Go to U Mass Boston and get some kinda accounting degree so he can work for his uncle's plumbing business."

"Leave me out of this." Sam, who'd been lying on his back, silently chewing on a long piece of grass, sat up at the mention of his name.

"What? I know you got an opinion. Come on, Sam. Jake's the best friend either of us is ever gonna have. You owe it to him to tell him what you told me."

Jake sat up now as well. His eyes narrow and hard. "Tell me what, Sam?"

"Nothing. I was just talking. Motormouth here

should keep his piehole shut. It didn't mean anything." Sam, who usually felt so relaxed with silence, shifted uncomfortably as Jake stared at him. "Okay, look, it was nothing. I just said the Air Force Academy is tough to get into, and I heard a lot of times you needed to have political pull, like having some congressman recommend you. Not a whole lot of members of Congress hanging around our neighborhood."

"So you don't think I can do it? You don't think I could get in?"

"Look, Jake, I'm sorry. I know you got dreams, and I think that's great. I'd just hate to see you set your sights on something that might be beyond your reach. Your grades are good. Really good. But I heard they've got to be near perfect to get into a school like the Air Force Academy."

Jake stood up and tugged my leash. "You know, you're something, Sam. You go days on end without stringing ten words together, and today you decide to tell me I'm wasting my time following my dream. Some friends you two turned out to be."

Jake gave my leash another tug, and we turned from the boys as Jake walked briskly away, kicking every rock he could find on the path. As we sped away, the boys called out to Jake, but he refused to look back or acknowledge them as they shouted out to him.

"Aw, c'mon on, Jake, I didn't mean anything!"

"Jake, don't be mad at me. I didn't say you couldn't do it. That was Sam. I just said I didn't want you to move that far away."

"Shut up, Dougie!"

"You shut up! Come on, Jake, we're sorry!"

Jake continued to shake his head, and we walked faster. He no longer searched for rocks to kick. Instead, he seemed to want to get as far away from the boys' voices as he could.

"Sam, Dougie, Skyler, none of them think I can do it. I'm telling you I can. I'm going to go to the Air Force Academy, and I'm going to fly jets, and nothing is going to stop me."

Jake continued talking to himself as he tugged at my leash, signaling me to run. My paws flew across the ground, my ears pinned against my head, and we raced away. Maria sat on her front steps and waved as we approached, but Jake didn't notice as we sped past her house.

When we got home, Jake unclipped my leash and went into his room, opening one of those books he seemed to like so much, staring at it and making marks on it until Mom called him to eat.

~ ~ ~ ~

After a few days, the boys started coming around again, and whatever they'd talked about that made Jake so angry seemed forgotten. But Jake had now changed in another way. Before, he used to look at his books and smile, humming to himself, but this was different. After that day, he'd stare at his books all day, talking to himself and marking the books, as if he were afraid he'd never see them again. So often, when the boys came by, they'd have to sit and wait while Jake continued staring at one of his books until that familiar smile lit his face. Then, finally, he'd put down his book, and we'd rush off with the boys, whooping and hollering, searching for our next adventure.

But sometimes, no amount of whining from Dougie or silent, dark stares from Sam could get Jake to leave his books, and the boys would slip away.

My Boy was searching for something, some big secret that seemed to elude him, but would he find his answers in those books he used to love but now seemed afraid to put down?

Maria's Story

I jumped up, barking before Maria knocked at the door. Her footsteps approaching our house and her fresh scent, a mixture of the soap she always used and whatever she had baked most recently, signaled her presence.

Maria came to visit all the time. She'd hug and talk with Mom before playing with me and, when he was around, hanging out with Jake. But Jake was around less and less.

"Sorry, Maria, but Jake's not here. I think he's gone to Skyler's for a swim."

"Oh, that's fine. I, ah . . . figured he'd be out. I just thought I'd come by and see if Bull was up for a walk. My brothers haven't seen him in days, and Diego especially misses him. Bull has such a wonderful calming effect on him."

My tail thumped at the sound of my name and the word *walk*. I couldn't resist. I jumped up and spun in a circle several times, barking to show my pleasure.

"Bull, sit."

I settled in front of my smiling friend and fidgeted impatiently, my tail rapidly wagging while Maria put my leash on.

I was sorry Jake wasn't with us. I loved it when we would go out together, my two friends laughing and pushing each other as they talked, but when alone with Maria, I'd get to run and run and run. Few things filled Maria with more joy than running. But first, we'd stop at her house.

I played with the boys until even Diego, content, fell exhausted on their worn couch. Then we walked on to the park, where Maria undid my leash and said, "Let's go, boy!"

Oh, how we ran. Maria couldn't run as fast as Jake, but she never tired. We raced around the field in loops again and again until my sides ached.

At last, perhaps out of kindness, Maria stopped the relentless pounding of her legs. I dropped to the ground with a contented huff, my tongue hanging from my mouth. Maria lay down next to me, her head resting on my side, and I panted, fighting to catch my breath.

Often, Maria lay there peacefully humming to herself or talking happily about that school place. But today, something was different. She cried softly and began to speak.

"Oh, Bull, what am I going to do? I've been crazy about him since I was five. And it's only gotten worse since I'm in high school too and have to see him with her every day. He can drive me crazy with his wisecracks and how he treats me like a little sister, but you see what a good person he is. Jake's so kind, with this almost naïve noble code of right and wrong that's just so admirable. So how can he be so blind? Why can't Jake see me, really *see me*, and understand how I feel about him? I see the way he looks at her. Why can't he look at me like that?"

We started walking back but stopped to sit on the bench I rested under when Jake and his friends played their games. With my head in Maria's lap, I licked her hand. I didn't want Maria to be so sad, but she sat there staring off into the empty field, as if she could see the boys playing. Like me, she must miss him very much.

Nothing would please me more than to be with Jake all the time, but humans expect more from the people they love than dogs do. Jake had changed and needed to be away sometimes. I would wait for him. Then, when he did come home, my job was to show him how much I missed him, hoping that might convince him to stay with the family who cared so much for him. But more and more, he got pulled away from us by school, spending time with Skyler, or this new word taking up so much of his time now: work.

But I didn't love him any less for going away. I always knew he'd come back to me. I wished I could tell Maria he'd come back to us, but I couldn't. So I nuzzled against her, trying to reassure her Jake loved us both and needed to be with us too. We had to be patient. But humans fail to see many things, and Maria was still very young. So she talked on about feelings I sensed we both shared.

"He acts like two years is this great divide. My mom was three years younger than my dad, and Mr. D is nearly ten years older than Mrs. D. Jake thinks Skyler is this Little Miss Perfect, self-controlled in her bubble, white-bread world. Oh, she's pretty, more than pretty, but I don't know . . . I just don't like her. Well, I guess I wouldn't like anybody Jake dated. But she just seems kind of empty, like there's nothing there behind all that fake charm and style.

"I just don't think she's right for him. She's trying to change him, to bring him into her circle of friends, getting him a job at her father's car dealership, pressuring him to spend less time with his old friends from the neighborhood, getting him to hang out at the county club. She seems so cool all the time, so aloof. Jake is passionate, full of life, while she sits back, watching, pretending to laugh or be involved while silently judging and wondering what words or actions will make her look the best. Jake is special, and Skyler doesn't even see it. She wants to change him, but we wouldn't want to change anything about the dummy. Well, maybe his taste in women."

Maria sighed, and tears ran down her face. "Oh, Bull, what would I do without you? You're the only one I can talk to. He's graduating at the end of the school year, and then he's off to college, following his dream to fly, and he'll forget I ever existed."

I brushed against her, trying to nudge my nose through her tightly folded hands, but nothing I did pulled Maria out of her dark mood. I had to be a bit of a *bad dog* to shake her out of her sadness. I jumped up, knocking Maria off the bench with my front paws, then I bowed in front of her, my head held low as I offered a friendly growl, inviting her to play. I barked and jumped from side to side until she called out to me, a broad smile on her face.

"Okay, the big fella wants to play."

With Maria giggling and shouting, she was ready for the chase. I darted off with my friend close behind. We ran and ran until even she was exhausted, and we went to lie in the tall grass on the hillside. Looking down upon the park, we fell asleep with the warm sun on our bodies. I woke to find Maria with her head resting on my side, and she began to hum, her sadness, at least for the moment, forgotten.

Life is good and full of pleasures. Dogs understand this, but our humans often need to be reminded. I was glad I could help Maria remember how good life was. Sure, Jake wasn't with us, but he was out there, and he'd come back.

At least, he always had before.

~ ~ ~ ~

Maria was back at our door, and like she often did, she had packages in her arms. Mom reached out to help and greeted her with a loving hug.

"How's your dad and the boys?"

"Fine. Papa says hello and thanks again for the manicotti. Said he doesn't know what we'd do without neighbors like you. I washed the tray and baked some biscotti for your family. Used the recipe you gave me, but making my mom's flan or empanadas still comes easier."

Mom smiled, reaching out to take a plate from Maria and close the door behind them.

"Give it time, honey. You've been cooking Cuban food since you were old enough to help your mother. I can still picture you standing on a chair to reach the kitchen counter, your eyes bright, attentively watching her every move. You've only been trying my Italian recipes for a few years. But you do seem especially inspired making any of *Jake's* favorites, ravioli, stuffed artichokes, bracciole."

"Why are you smiling? No . . . oh nooo, is it that obvious?" Maria's voice rose, her eyes unable to meet Mom's.

Mom reached out and took Maria's hand. "Maria, darling, it's been obvious since you were six years old, and Jake squirted you with the garden hose. Remember? You told him he was the ugliest boy God ever made."

"I'm so embarrassed. Please, tell me Jake doesn't know."

"Don't worry. He may not be the ugliest boy God ever made, but he's a teenage boy, and God made most of them pretty dumb when it comes to affairs of the heart. Our boy Jake is right up near the front of the clueless pack."

"What can I do? He either treats me like his kid sister or looks right through me. It's all about Skyler. 'I'm going over Skyler's. Did I tell you what Skyler said? Did you see Skyler's new car?' I know I shouldn't say this, but I just don't think she's good enough for him."

"Be patient, honey. Life's full of surprises, with lots of twists and turns. Who knows what's meant to be? You're both young, and even if Jake is the one, you both need to experience life beyond this side of town before you settle down. Now, enough about obtuse teenage boys. How are you?"

Mom and Maria walked into the kitchen, where

Mom put the plate Maria had brought with the sweet, nutty treats on the table and got them both a drink. They sat and talked while they nibbled on Maria's treats and other goodies Mom put out. Maria's mood swung quickly from sad to happy, anxious to relaxed. I sat by her side as Maria petted me, scratching behind my ears and talking while Mom listened in her attentive, relaxed style.

"I'm good, Mrs. D. Busy, like always, with school stuff and work around the house. Papa's swamped too. I try to do everything I can to help, but he doesn't want me tied to the house. Papa keeps insisting I stay in the church choir, track, and work on the school paper. He's so proud. You'd think I'm the first sophomore ever to win a cross-country meet or take first place in the high school science fair. I told him I was thinking about quitting cross-country, and he went through the roof. You know how calm he usually is. But he got furious and told me I should never quit something I love. He said running and choir were the only times he saw me looking completely relaxed. I love him for it, but there's just so much to do at home. Diego is getting bigger *and* stronger, and only a handful of people outside my family and yours, Bull included, can calm him down when he gets nervous or scared. The twins try, but they're still so young, and I want them to have a childhood–"

"Stop right there."

I stirred. Mom's firm voice demanded attention. That special voice said she wanted something and wasn't going to take no for an answer. The same voice that told me I better drop the ball I had in my mouth and pay attention. When she used that tone, Jake and Dad knew there'd be no sense arguing. Mom had made up her mind.

Yes, when Mom sounded like that, everyone stopped and listened.

"You are sixteen years old, young lady. I don't know why God works the way he does. Why he chose to take your mother when you were only ten years old, leaving your father with a special-needs son, a young daughter, and twins just out of diapers. But he did.

"I saw you grow up almost overnight from a carefree little girl into a young woman taking on responsibilities at your house. I wept, thinking how proud your mother would be, and how sad. Life forced you to grow up too early. I've tried to help out, but I haven't done a thing your mother wouldn't have done for my family. So listen, there is no way I'll stand by and watch your childhood slip away. Your mother was a rare and loving person. She helped me through multiple miscarriages and tried so hard to keep me from feeling bad when she was pregnant with the twins, knowing I'd just lost a baby."

Mom's voice changed, and she shifted in her chair. I lifted my head from Maria's lap and saw sadness in Mom's eyes, like I'd seen when I first came to live with my family so long ago.

"I never told you this, but the last time I visited your mother in the hospital, all she did was talk about you kids. I never saw anybody fight harder. She wanted so badly to be there for you all. But finally, she knew this was one battle she couldn't win. She found peace that night. Her time had come, and she was ready to let go. She just wanted to be sure you kids would be okay.

"I promised her I'd be there for you all, and I've tried my very best. John and I love you kids like you are our own, and there's no way I'll let you miss out on one high school experience. You deserve nothing less, and you'll have your father *and me* to deal with if I hear you talking again of quitting cross-country or anything else you love. Understood?"

Maria looked up to meet Mom's determined eyes. "Yes, ma'am. And thanks. Knowing your family is there for us means the world to me. I don't know if I should say this, but I remember when the twins were born. You were always helping. One day I saw you feeding fussy Carlos a bottle while José slept, and you were crying. I asked my mom afterward why you were sad. She said you just had a baby go to heaven, and you missed her. She told me you may never have a little girl of your own, and I should always think of you as my second mother because she knew how much you loved me."

Mom reached across the table and took Maria's hands. "She told you that? And you've remembered it all these years? You weren't more than eight. Your mother was a wonderful person, and she was right. You are like a daughter to me, and I couldn't have asked for a more lovely one.

"Your mother was my dear friend, and I miss her every day. The only thing that eases the pain is I get to see her every time I look at you. With each passing day, you remind me of her more and more. I know she is watching, and I know she's very proud of you."

Maria and Mom hugged each other, and they began to cry. It wasn't a real sad crying because they smiled too.

Sometimes I don't understand humans, why they laugh or cry, but I understand when a family is in love. I sighed. Content, I nuzzled closer to Maria. Our family was very much in love.

Another Christmas

It was cold, colder than the day I came home to live with my family. The sharp air clung to my nose, and I remembered the day Jake brought me home holding me ever so tightly against his warm body, protecting me from the icy weather. Despite the bright sun, I'd snuggled deeply, his thick coat zipped up around both of us, shielding me from biting wind and a painful freezing air I'd never known before.

Until that day, I'd only known the warmth of my mother and siblings' bodies as we nursed. The biting wind that first day cautioned me of things I didn't yet understand. In time, I recognized the changes coming in my life and understood the weather often signaled these changes. So with the arrival of the cold air and the now-familiar activities around me, I could tell we were having another one of those big parties I enjoyed so much.

Crazy humans, we had a tree in our house again, and everyone ran in and out carrying all kinds of packages. The smell of food drifted throughout our home while my nose twitched and drool flowed from my mouth, wetting the floor. I stayed close to

Mom and Dad while they worked together, cooking up all kinds of tasty delights, and I gobbled up every bit of food that fell to the ground.

Those evil giant bugs were back again. I cautiously eyed them as they rattled around the large pot, their claws sticking out in search of freedom. I stayed far away, watching Mom expertly pick them up, carefully avoiding those snappy pinchers. I'd learned my lesson. I didn't plan on getting my nose anywhere near those powerful bugs, and it amazed me how easily Mom handled them. All grown up and much better prepared to do battle if they escaped, I was still proud of Mom's skills and pleased I wouldn't have to face those angry claws again.

I lay on the floor, smelling all the wonderful fish smells cooking while Dad sang to Mom as she happily busied herself with all her preparations. I could tell this would be a fun night with lots of food, family, and friends filling our house with laughter. Big parties meant lots of belly scratches, special attention, and not-so-accidentally dropped food for me. I closed my eyes to doze, but my nose stayed alert for any falling treats.

No one rang the bell, which was usually my signal to bark, announcing we had visitors. No, on these special nights, people just walked in with their food in hand, hugging and kissing my family while Mom struggled to find a spot to put the food they'd brought. If Mom was lucky, they'd be carrying things to drink, and she wouldn't have to find room on the tables or counters. Instead, she could direct them to the big ice chest kept in that little back room. It seemed so long since I'd stayed there as a puppy. My tail beat against our visitors as I walked through the crowd, enjoying our special night.

Everyone came. Maria and her family and lots of other neighbors. Sam and Dougie were there. Even Nonna and Nonno had come from the place called Florida with Uncle Tommy and Auntie Karen, who now lived there too. This year, Auntie Karen had a tiny human with her. They called her Baby Gina, and everyone cautioned me to be gentle. But I could already tell this tiny human was helpless. So I was the Best Boy I could be, even as Baby Gina reached out with her chubby little hands to grab my ear or poke at my eyes.

Some people only stayed long enough to have a little something to eat before going back out into the bitter cold air. But others visited long into the night, eating and laughing. Skyler came, and Jake got all excited, introducing her to any of the people she didn't already know. Everyone was loud and laughing, giving her lots of hugs and kisses. Lucky Skyler. Uncle Tommy kept repeating, "*Che bella regazza bionda,*" which I didn't understand, but it brought approving nods from Nonno and sharp pokes in Uncle Tommy's side from Auntie Karen.

Skyler smiled widely while her eyes moved rapidly around the room, but she didn't seem very relaxed with all the noise and activity. That smile of hers stayed locked all night. Shifting from one leg to the other, Skyler managed to slip away from the attention. Jake found her and sat next to her on the couch. I followed and sat at his feet, enjoying the warmth of our house. My belly now long since full, I just wanted to be with My Boy.

"What's it your grandparents keep calling you? Gia-what?"

"Giacomo."

"Yes, Giaco . . . Yes, that. Why do they keep calling you that?"

"It's my name. I was baptized Giacomo DiSpirito. Giacomo means Jacob in Italian. My friends all call me Jake, but sometimes my parents, and especially my older relatives, call me Giacomo." Jake smiled as he spoke. "It's like with my Dad. His real name is Giovanni, and most people call him John, but his mom and old friends from the neighborhood still call him Giovanni or just Gio. I think it's sorta cool that we've got the best of both worlds. We've kept the old traditions while embracing all the changes around us."

"Traditions, you mean like tonight, the way you all celebrate Christmas Eve?"

"Well, yes. We celebrate lots of days. Easter and feast days, like Saint Joseph's. My mother's mom's name is Giuseppina. It means Josephine in Italian." Jake's voice sounded excited, like when we were learning a new trick or when he talked to Maria about one of those books he was always holding. "The Feast of Saint Joseph is a big day for her. When they still lived up here, Uncle Tommy always went to Fisichilli's Bakery on her Feast Day to buy zeppole. It's her favorite pastry. Don't know what they do in Florida, but I bet Uncle Tommy figured something out.

"Yeah, lots of holidays, but Christmas Eve is probably the biggest. Why, aren't you having fun?" After an evening filled with joy, Jake's voice no longer matched the happiness of the people around him.

"Sure, it's all very nice. And please don't get defensive, but . . . don't you think it's all a bit too much?"

"Not sure what you mean by *too much*. But big parties like this are common in the Flats, whether Italians, Poles, Latinos, or, more recently, Vietnamese. Around here, you're going to find lots of food, friends, and family celebrating."

Skyler kept shifting on the couch, acting like I did when Dad first wanted me to sleep in our cloth house when we went camping.

"And so much noise. Don't be mad, but it's a lot to take. Everyone's hugging, kissing, arguing. And the food. I've never seen so much, with more fish than I could ever imagine."

Jake laughed, perhaps hoping to chase away Skyler's anxiousness. "Well, it's not really arguing. It's just passionate people with lots of opinions. Mom says Italians are the only people in the world who can have two guys in a room arguing three different points of view. You should see my Uncle Frank and Uncle Tommy when they get going. Who was better, DiMaggio or Williams, Ali or Marciano? It would make your head spin.

"As for the food. Come to our house, and you're not leaving hungry. The seafood is just part of an old Italian tradition. On Christmas Eve, we celebrate the Feast of the Seven Fishes and prepare all kinds of seafood specialties. The menu varies, and each home has its personal favorites. For my family, there are a few non-negotiables. Mom always makes lobster *fra diavolo*. That's lobsters in tomato sauce, probably my favorite. We also have to have my Nonna Connie's calamari and her stuffed clams. Then Mom makes the smelliest, saltiest fish dish in the world called bacala. You have to soak it for days, and it stinks up the house for a week, but it wouldn't be Christmas for my father's dad if he didn't get his bacala. He died a few years ago, but Mom's still making it." Jake reached out to take Skyler's hand and smiled, but his eyes showed only sadness.

"Come on, Skyler, I'm sure you've got Christmas traditions at your house."

"Oh, sure. Before my father moved out for good a few years ago, he'd buy my mother some gaudy piece of jewelry and give me a check. Then we'd go to Indian Ridge for steaks and Lobster Thermidor."

"I'm sorry."

"Don't be." Skyler's voice was hard and cold. "I got used to it, and I'm not sure I can handle all this activity, to tell you the truth. It's nice, but I'm too private a person for all this. I'm more of a steak at the country club kind of girl anyway."

I rose from the floor and brushed across Skyler's leg, but she didn't stir. Surrounded by all the laughter and people, she sat, unsmiling, the same plate of untouched food resting in her lap. Talking only to Jake, she continued to look around the room, perhaps searching for a way to escape. I couldn't tell if Jake noticed because he too grew silent, as if he'd run out of things to say. Like the party had lost its joy for him.

While Jake and Skyler grew more silent, the

laughter from the others rose, and the house grew louder. Dad held Mom in his arms, spinning her around the room while the older people clapped their hands and sang out in strange, fast-paced words:

"*C'è 'na la luna mezz'u mare, Mamma mia m'a maretare. Figlia mia a cu te dare Mamma mia pensace tu . . .*"

Everyone laughed, continuing to clap their hands, especially Nonna and Nonno from Florida and Nonna Connie. Jake stepped over me, leading Skyler away from all the noise and laughter that filled the room. I watched them slip out of the house into the cold night air and away from all the joy.

Why would anyone walk away from so much happiness and love?

A Troubled Friend

The terrible cold slowly passed, and the warmer weather brought wonderful smells waffling through our open windows. Jake grabbed my leash, hooked it onto his bike, and with a smile on his face, shouted out, "Come on, Bull, let's go. I'm not working at the dealership today and gotta make some money. Can't let my girl drive me around town in her car for the rest of my life. I've got a senior prom to pay for."

This had become a common way we'd spend our day when Jake was not at school or the workplace Skyler talked about so much. So, with my leash tied to Jake's bike, I ran up the Hill to where Skyler lived, a place with big houses surrounded by tall trees.

Tied to his bike, I'd watch Jake knock on the door of one house after another to talk to the people living in these big homes. Sometimes they'd only speak for a few moments before we'd move on, but other times they'd talk longer. When Jake took off his jacket, it was my signal to curl up and relax. We would be there for a while. Jake worked like he did with Dad around the house. He'd push some noisy machine back and forth across the grass or dig holes using a stick with a big shiny edge. Jake moved plants around people's yards like Mom moved furniture in the house.

But no matter how busy he got, Jake always checked to see if I needed anything. He'd walk me to the nearest tree for me to do my business and let me drink from the long rope with its bubbling water. Drinking took longer this way than from a bowl, but I loved gulping at the fast-flowing stream. I'd snap at it, gurgling as if it were alive and wanted to play. Jake would smile, watching me drink, and when my thirst was gone, he'd run the water over my back, neck, and chest to help keep me cool.

This day my friend Anthony came shuffling up the hill, wearing the shirt he always wore. He called the shirt and his big black boots his "uniform." Anthony was a big man and dark, darker even than Jake or Maria after they had been out in the hot sun all summer. And like Jake, Anthony's hair was tight like a poodle's, only much more so.

Anthony walked up the street, his head down, talking to himself like he often did. Anthony usually lived in a big house not far from our home. Lots of other people lived there or went there to eat. My family visited this place a lot. They called it *volunteering,* and they often took me with them to say hello to all the people. Everyone there was always happy to see me, and it pleased me when someone who moments before had been acting anxious or angry stopped to smile when I greeted them.

Like many people at the large house, Anthony

didn't like staying inside. Maybe he felt like I did out in the woods with my family. Maybe being stuck inside the house made him nervous, like having to stay in the cloth house made me. I think it was times like these when I'd see Anthony wandering around our neighborhood with his blanket on his back. Everyone near our home knew Anthony and was used to seeing him walking around, sitting in the park, or talking to himself. But today was the first time I'd seen him up on the Hill surrounded by all the big houses.

My tail thumped wildly the moment I saw him. Anthony always had time to stop and say hello, and he often had food in the bag he carried to share with me. Despite the goodies and how nice he always treated me, Anthony was filled with sadness and needed someone to be with. I tried to be that someone, and it pleased me to help. Sometimes Anthony shouted at people or hit himself in the head, scolding himself for things I never quite understood. I'm not sure anyone did, but you could tell he wouldn't really hurt anyone, even when he was acting mad and yelling. He was just alone and scared.

No matter how upset Anthony became, getting to be with me and pet me helped him relax. Dad and Jake knew this too, so they'd always stop to talk to Anthony and let me say hello. When Anthony had problems walking or standing up, Dad would calmly talk to Anthony, convincing him to get in the car with us, and we'd buy him something to eat. If Anthony was very upset and we couldn't calm him down, Dad took him to a different place, a much bigger house far away from where we lived. Dad would go inside with him and somehow convince Anthony to stay and visit the people there. Anthony always looked better the next time we saw him after visiting this big house. His clothes were clean, he'd have no problems walking or standing up, and he'd be calmer and more relaxed. But in time, he'd slip and become sad again.

Today was a good day. Anthony wasn't shouting or hitting himself. I barked hello, and he smiled. With his head down, Anthony ran across the street to see me. Not looking, he stepped in front of a car driving very fast down the quiet road. A terrible screech hurt my ears, and Anthony jumped out of the way, falling to the ground as the car stopped well past where Anthony lay on the ground, shaking.

Like Skyler's, this car didn't have a roof. A group of boys a little older than Jake jumped out of the car without opening the doors to yell at Anthony.

"Watch where ya going, General!"

"What are you doing up on the Hill anyway?"

Frightened for Anthony, I barked my warning bark while the angry boys walked toward him, shouting. Anthony sat on the ground crying, his face buried in his hands as I continued to bark, the fur rising on my back. I was afraid these boys would hurt Anthony, or he could fall into one of his sad moods and hurt himself.

Jake saw what happened and raced over to put himself between Anthony and the three older boys.

"Do we have a problem, guys?"

"Mind your business, DiSpirito. G. I. Joe over

here ran in front of my car like some lunatic. I don't know what halfway house or VA clinic he comes from, but he doesn't belong up here. The Hill's private security shoulda spotted him and *escorted* him down to the other side of town."

"His name is Anthony, and he served two tours in Iraq. He's having a bit of a hard time since he got home, but he's fine if he stays on his meds. I'll take him with me and."

Jake spoke calmly, and I stopped barking, the fur on my back slowly dropping. It seemed he had gotten everyone to calm down. But then Anthony jumped up and started shouting, "Free country! Free country!"

I smelled his fear as Anthony shuffled from side to side. He moved toward the three boys and shouted, "You're bad people! Bad people!"

Jake stepped in front of Anthony to stop him. But as Jake stood with his calming hands on Anthony's shoulders, the biggest of the three boys, an angry-looking boy with long yellow hair, turned on Anthony and hit him, knocking him down. While Anthony lay on the ground, the angry boy began kicking my fallen friend.

Jake tackled the taller boy, dragging him to the ground, and was quickly on top of him, holding him pinned down.

"He's sick, man! What's the matter with you?"

I started barking again, my deep, angry bark, hoping someone older, like Mom or Dad, would come along and get everyone to behave. But unlike our neighborhood, where people were always out, walking or sitting on their front steps talking to neighbors, you never seemed to see any of the people who lived in these big houses.

With Jake on top of the bigger boy, Anthony sat on the curb, rocking back and forth and crying. I hoped the worst was over, but the other boys pulled Jake off their friend and held him while the bigger boy with the yellow hair hit Jake again and again.

I'd never done anything more aggressive than growl at a stranger who smelled like they couldn't be trusted and never thought I'd ever attack a human. But seeing Anthony sitting on the curb crying while these older boys hurt My Boy, I had to protect them. I stopped barking and raced into the street, dragging the bike behind me. I jumped onto the tall boy, knocking him to the ground, and stood over him, the fur on my back now straight up. With my front paws on his chest and my fangs bared, I stared into his pale eyes, growling with an anger I'd never known before.

"Bull, heel!"

Jake's command rang out, but I wouldn't get off until Jake and Anthony were safe. I stood there growling and stared into the frightened eyes of the bigger boy who just moments before had been hitting Jake while his friends held back the arms of the boy I loved.

"Bull, heel!" Jake repeated his command.

I looked up. He and Anthony were now safe. The other boys had jumped away, the fear showing on their faces as they hurried back toward their car. I stepped off and backed away slowly, my eyes locked on the tall boy as I continued to growl with a wave of rage I didn't know I possessed.

"Come on, Kyle, let's get the hell outta here!" one of the other boys called out.

"You don't belong up here on the Hill, DiSpirito. You or your cousin over there. I don't know what Skyler sees in you, but it's just a matter of time before she kicks your lowlife, broke ass to the curb!"

The other boys were now at their car and yelling for their friend to join them. I stepped back farther but continued to growl, watching the last boy scramble away.

He shouted as he ran. "You'll never belong up here, you or that rabid mutt of yours!"

He jumped into the back of the car, and with smelly smoke rising around it, the car made that painful screeching sound again. As they drove off, the tall boy stood up in the car and threw a bottle that smashed on the ground, spreading shattered glass across the street.

I walked over to Anthony, the bike still dragging behind me. I lay down beside him and nuzzled against my friend until he stopped crying. We stayed like that a long time, and at last, he began to breathe regularly. Anthony slowly calmed, and I thought how lucky we all were Jake was there. Anthony could never deliberately hurt anyone, but resting my head in his lap as Anthony hugged me, I again felt how powerfully built he was. If pushed too far, Anthony could have badly hurt those boys who'd been so mean to him.

Like Old Times

I rode in the car, my face out the window, the rush of the wind and tantalizing smells whooshing past me as my flapping ears beat against my head. We made several stops to pick up our friends. First, Maria and Diego's house. Then Sam's, and finally Dougie's. It had been a long time since I'd seen the boys, and I could smell everyone's excitement at being together again.

The small car overflowed with our young friends, and I had to sit on Sam's lap on the ride. Sam groaned and kept trying to get me to lie on the floor at his feet. But I was too eager, enjoying the smells and sounds, to move from my spot by the window. So I rode on, surrounded by noisy, joy-filled young people. Soon, the scent of saltwater filled the air. We were going to the big crashing water. I loved the crashing water, and my tail whipped madly in anticipation.

"Pretty sweet, our man Jake. The first in our crew to get a car, and he christens it by taking his best friends to the beach. Look at that cool fighter pilot's dexterity managin' the wheel of this state-of-the-art piece of equipment." Dougie stopped and smiled. "Our boy Jake said he could do it, and he did. Number three in our class. The Air Force Academy has to notice. I'll miss him, but, hey, our country is in good hands with such skilled young men guardin' our skies and roads."

"Stop!" Sam's deep voice shook the car while Dougie's constant yipping distracted him, at least for the moment, from his efforts to make me lie on the floor. "Between you and this drooling giant sitting in my lap, I've had enough. Just stop talking!"

"No can do. Look at this place, *Alphabet Man*. Glorious Hampton Beach. The sun is shinin', and we're only minutes away from buryin' our toes in the warm sand. The Four Musketeers: Jake, Sam, the noble Diego Fuentes, and of course, yours truly, the ever-heroic and dashin' Dougie Donovan. We're together again, with the lovely Maid Maria by our side. The world is ours for the tastin', and we're gonna go forth and devour... "

"That's it! I'm gonna hurt you!" Sam's powerful voice momentarily silenced Dougie. "I swear it, seems no one can shut you up, even under threat of a serious beating. But Dougie, I beg you. If you ever, *ever* meet a woman who can get you to stop talking, please, please, please marry her!"

"Never gonna happen, Sam, my man. I have too much joy and wisdom to share with the world, and share it,I must. It's like Butch said to the Sundance Kid. 'I got vision, and the rest of the world wears bifocals.'"

Dougie was doing that thing with his voice, making himself sound like different people. Sometimes it was Jake or Sam, or sometimes he sounded like some fancy person I didn't know. These voices could make people laugh while other times they'd groan. But if his friends were reacting, Dougie seemed filled with glee.

"It would be wrong for me to deny others access to all the pearls racin' through this world-class mind of mine. In fact, word is the fellas down the road at Harvard have heard about me up in this tired old mill town and would like me to come to Cambridge and speak to them. You know, sort of a professor emeritus kinda thing. I'm thinkin' I might stop off at Fenway to watch the Sox and make a day of it."

The smell of the salt grew stronger, and I could see the crashing water while Dougie continued with his Jack Russell, yipping about just what, I'm not sure. Jake stopped the car, and Dougie, still talking, jumped out, followed quickly by Sam chasing him around the car, shouting in his powerful voice, "Stop, or I'm gonna make you!"

My ears pricked upward. Might Sam actually hurt Dougie this time? But Dougie, unconcerned, wouldn't stop yipping away.

"Half a league, half a league, half a league onward. Blah, blah, blah. Death Valley rode the six hundred. See that, Jakie, you thought I didn't listen when you talked about all those poems you like so much."

Dougie stopped for a moment to look at Jake and smiled brightly. Then he was gone, chattering away as he ran to the water, eluding the grasp of Sam, who raced after him. Maria, appearing a little worried about Dougie's safety, attached my leash and called to me. I jumped out of the car and felt the sun's heat coming up through the pads of my paws as we ran across the sandy beach to the deserted spot where Dougie and Sam had dropped blankets for everyone. But the boys were already gone. They'd run off to wrestle in the water. So Maria spread blankets for the others, leaving me to dig a deep hole to help keep me cool.

I looked up to see Jake alone with Diego, as he often was. Jake had his arm around Diego, and they were smiling, walking side by side toward the water.

"Jake, the place is nearly empty. Let's unleash the hound and let Bull play in the surf before a lifeguard shows up and the beach gets too crowded."

Dougie, still dripping wet from his swim, removed my leash while he spoke, and together we ran back to the water with the others right behind us. Sam picked up a stick as he ran, and the boys took turns tossing it out deep, beyond the rough, foamy white water.

On the shore, Jake showed Diego how to hold the stick so he too could throw it far out over the rushing water, out to where it was smooth and still. Diego grabbed the stick and reached back slowly, tossing it just past the rushing water, and shouted with delight as Jake clapped his hands, celebrating Diego's success.

I was off. Joyfully, I fought my way through the foam-filled rapids to the far-off stick. Once in my mouth, I turned around to be pulled toward the shore, guided back by the mighty rushing water, back to the cheering boys. With my head held high,

I dropped the stick at their feet and gave a triumphant shake, making Diego squeal in excitement.

I stood tall, intently barking as I looked at them, signaling I was ready to gallop back out over the choppy water to do it all again.

It was wonderful, and I almost never tired of playing this game. But finally, panting and thirsty, I was ready to rest. With my tongue hanging loosely, I followed Jake back to the blanket. I lapped up water Jake poured into a bowl he'd brought and looked up contently while he refilled the now-empty bowl. Then, with my thirst satisfied, I went back to work digging while Dougie, Maria, and Diego continued playing in the water. I plopped myself into my cool, freshly dug hole, and Sam's voice rose above the crashing water.

"I'm really proud of you, Jake. You worked your butt off, and your dream is within your grasp. But I hope you don't let something even more important slip away while you chase that dream."

Jake turned to look at his friend. "Okay, Silent Sam, you obviously have something more to say. What is it?"

Sam's face grew even more serious than usual, and he pointed down toward the water where the others continued to play. "You better make your move soon, DiSpirito, or you're gonna lose that girl."

"What are you talking about?"

"What am I talking about? Well, you're either blind or stupid if you can't see it. Maybe you've had your nose buried in all those books or writing your stories. Our sweet little Maria Fuentes has grown up, and she's not only one of the best-looking girls in town, but she is also a terrific kid. Oh, but wait . . . You're gonna tell me you hadn't noticed."

"Hey, I have eyes, but Maria's like a kid sister to us all."

Jake scratched behind my ear as he spoke, but his touch lacked its usual calm as Sam continued talking.

"Well, take a look at Dougie down there. He's taking every opportunity he can to be with Maria. It doesn't look like Dougie thinks he's hanging out with his sister. I'd probably be there too, but I always figured you two belonged together. It's been that way since we were kids. Long as I can remember, I figured she was the one for you. But if you insist on staying with that Ice Princess up on the Hill, you're gonna lose that girl with the big heart, and it might just be to me. God knows that knucklehead Dougie doesn't stand a chance with a girl like Maria."

"I swear, Sam, sometimes I wonder about you. You can go hours without saying a friggin' word, and now you're talking crazy. You know I'm with Skyler."

"Tick tock, Jakie Boy. Tick tock."

I stirred, surprised by the tone in Jake's voice. But Sam smiled, his eyes bright. He lay back on the blanket and rested his large hands behind his head, contentedly humming to himself. Typical for Sam, he didn't speak again for a long time, but Jake seemed bothered by something the rest of the day.

Through all this, Dougie was Dougie. He

wouldn't stop moving, talking, and teasing everyone, mostly Maria. It wasn't till our ride home, with everyone exhausted from playing all day in the water, that even Dougie finally grew quiet.

Still, Jake didn't act like his typical happy self as we dropped everyone off one by one. The last stop was Maria's house. She and Diego left tired and smiling but with barely a goodbye from Jake. As they faded away up the walk toward their house, Jake's faint voice hung in the air.

"Tick tock."

PART III

The Long Journey

My nose twitched, and my eyes flickered open. The smell of Mom's cooking woke me from a dead sleep. In the darkness, footsteps fell softly on the floor, and Dad hurried by, carrying the sacks we take when we go into the woods. He grabbed the long poles with the strings attached, and my tail began to thump. Dad and Jake used those poles to catch the fish they'd heat over an open fire when we stayed away for days. It was a sign this would be a long trip.

My tail swished back and forth, and I barked my approval, following Jake through the house. He grabbed our cloth house, putting it in the car, and I ran after him, brushing my side against his leg.

I sensed the next few days would be special, but I had no hint of the danger we were about to face and the bond of love we'd seal forever on this fateful trip.

After a long drive, I raced to a cluster of trees to do some business. I marked many spots before running back to the car, ready to explore.

"It's been a dry, hot summer, and our usual fishing spots have probably been picked clean. What do you say to hiking up off the beaten trail? I know a small lake about another ten miles in from our usual place."

Dad helped Jake strap on one of the sacks while he spoke. Dad had that look in his eyes, like when he'd been thinking long about something important.

"The trails are rough and aren't well-traveled, and the bugs at night are merciless. But it's one of the prettiest spots I know, with the best fishing you could imagine. So, what do you think? Are you and your pup up for a bit of a hike?"

"You lead the way, old man. Bull and I will keep up."

"Hah, *old man*, is it? We'll see who's dragging their tails in a few hours."

We didn't stop at any of the regular places for Jake and Dad to set up our cloth house for the night. No, we pushed on and on. We walked so far, I lost the scent of many of the things I knew so well. There were no hints of cars, houses, or other people, but incredible new smells replaced them. All kinds of animals, some familiar, but others entirely new. Climbing far into the thick, dark woods, I sniffed all this and much more.

We walked on far from what we knew, and I quickly recognized where unfortunate animals had been captured and eaten by others bigger or quicker than they. My legs trembled as I sniffed the spots. I smelled the markings of many animals and found food caches where they burrowed away supplies for future needs. The smells were incredible and exciting, but I trembled again, the fur rising on my back at these strange scents. These were animals I'd never seen before, and the bloody smell of fresh kills and the markings left behind told me many were large and dangerous.

I found signs of a big cat, larger than anything I'd ever imagined, and I stopped, my fur rising higher as I lowered my nose to study the smell of another animal who concerned me even more. I could tell this last beast was very large, bigger than me, bigger than Dad, and I walked on alertly, fearing the power one of these animals would possess. With my ears up and my nose twitching for more signs, I searched for lurking dangers while I moved through these beautiful woods with my two favorite men trailing behind me.

We stopped several times for Jake to give me water from the bottle he carried in his sack. On breaks, we sat under giant trees that blocked the sun, enjoying just being together. Dogs don't want much from the people we love. The ability to run free, a belly rub or scratch behind the ear, and the pleasure of their companionship are all we need. This trip was giving me all of this and much more.

After a long, hot walk, we came to a clearing, and the darkness of the thick trees opened to a sunlit field of tall grass. A small stream jaggedly crossed the hillside where the water flowed quickly past us through the clearing. At the bottom of the hill, the stream came to rest in a flat, still lake. I was hot and tired. I didn't look to Jake or Dad for permission but ran down the hillside as fast as I could toward the cool, clear water.

With my ears pinned behind me, I headed for a

flock of large white birds feeding in the shallow end of the lake where the stream brought its icy water. My tail held high, I hurried toward the birds, forcing them to fly off in a huff, squawking in annoyance. I knew I wouldn't catch them, but I made a show of chasing them off the flat, still lake and up into flight. I raised my paw with my tail stuck out straight behind me as they flew off. Their flapping wings filled the sky. I sensed forcing these birds into flight was one of my jobs when with my humans.

The birds gone, I jumped into the water, making a loud splash. It was colder than any water I'd ever been in, but I snorted with pleasure. It felt wonderful. With my paws moving lazily and my head held high, I swam through the welcoming water. Refreshed, I paddled back to where Jake and Dad stood and shook myself dry while Jake laughed, shouting for me to stay back. I began running around them in circles, and I barked with a friendly growl as I bowed, my head held low, moving side to side in an invitation to play. Jake found a stick and threw it into the water for me to swim out to and bring back. Again, again.

I could have played all day, but there was work to do. So, with one last shake, I walked off to do my part in preparing our camp for the night. Jake and Dad busied themselves putting up our cloth house and collecting wood for a fire before going to the edge of the quiet lake, bringing their sticks with the strings attached. At the water's edge, they performed their ritual. Carefully, they'd swing their sticks back and forth before casting the string far out over the water, where it landed far from the noise and activity. There, in the deepest part of the lake, their lines flowed through the water, searching for where the fish might be largest and most abundant.

While they did this, I explored the area around our camp. I wanted to know who or what had been there recently and what dangers these recent visitors could bring. Dad certainly picked a good spot for us to find fish. The scent of fish caught in this spot in recent days was everywhere, but something alarmed me. There was no scent of humans. Instead, it was the big animal I'd noticed earlier in the day. The smell of the beast was strong, and it was clear he'd been coming to this far-off spot to feed on the fish that flowed so plentifully from the nearby stream. The longer I explored, the more uncomfortable I became. The giant beast had been spending a lot of time here. Dad caught a large fish and put it in the basket near his feet while I continued investigating. Soon Jake shouted, his voice childlike in excitement, announcing he too had a fish on the end of his string, which he expertly maneuvered, pulling it slowly ever closer toward the shore and the waiting basket.

After discovering the markings and scent of the giant beast, I didn't like this spot much anymore. Despite the abundance of fish, I wanted to leave. But I knew with our cloth house set up and supper ready to be cooked, we would be there for the night. Dad and Jake had done their part in building our house, finding supper, and making a fire for the night. The rest was my job. I'd need to be on guard for any danger the darkness brought. I'd be watching for the large cat and the even more mysterious giant beast who'd been coming here in recent days to feed.

Like dogs or cats, this beast spent most of its time on four paws. Curiously, though, around a tall bush with berries, I could tell it had walked on its back paws like humans as it picked at the fruit high up in the bush. But no matter how it walked, I could tell it was big, and I didn't like being near its feeding area. I only hoped Dad and Jake had seen the potential dangers so evident to me. But, whether they had or not, I'd stay on guard, watchful through the night, making sure the people I loved were not surprised by the looming menace.

The Scent of Danger

"You weren't lying, Dad. Great spot, The fish were jumping onto our hooks

Sure were. This lake's off the beaten path, and it gets cool at night come the end of summer. Most folks aren't willing to fight their way up here. But the fishing makes it worth the effort."

We'd eaten our fill, and Dad poked the fire with a stick while he continued talking. "We need to be careful, though. I've seen lots of tracks, coyotes, bobcats, and a bear. The bear, in particular, may not appreciate the company. Best we don't interact or tempt them. Let's keep a good-sized and well-banked fire through the night, bury our food scraps far outside camp, and keep whatever food we have sealed tightly in the mini-cooler."

"Agreed. Bear attacks are rare, but no sense tempting fate."

"Yep, this is their home, not ours. We're the guest. If we're respectful of that and don't frighten them, we should be okay. But you can easily spook a bear in isolated spots like this. You're plenty experienced, but remember, when hiking anywhere bears could be, it's important we make lots of noise. We want them to know we're nearby. They get aggressive when surprised. Winter's coming. They have to fatten up before hibernation, and they'll be more aggressive searching for food."

"Check out Bull."

"He knows something's up." As he spoke, Dad leaned over to scratch the thick fur high up on my chest. "Look at him, head held high, ears perked, nostrils flared. Never seen him so intent. He'll let us know if anything approaches the camp. We just need to be on the alert. It's clear Bull is."

I sat between Dad and Jake. My tail thumped at Dad mentioning my name, and Jake moved closer to run his hand across my back. At home, I might've rolled over and offered my belly for some tummy scratches, but we weren't home. We were in a strange place. A place I didn't know. This was no time to relax. Accepting the loving strokes, I stared off past the darkening camp. With my head high, I perked my ears as my eyes opened wider, and my nose twitched, searching for danger. Despite the heat from the fire, I felt cold, and I curled up next to Jake, sharing in his warmth as I had with my siblings so long ago.

"I'm glad we did this. It seems we get away less each year. I'm afraid it won't be long before we don't get out at all."

"Sorry, Dad, I'm just so busy these days."

"Don't be. I'm happy you have so much happening: School, sports, friends, new job. But I want you to know how much I enjoy spending time with you. You're busy, but your Mom and I are always there for you and love the time we spend with you."

"Something you just said made me think. Can I ask you something?"

"Always."

Jake stopped petting me as he put his hands together and rested them under his chin, elbows on his knees, staring into the fire, then turned to look at Dad.

"When you listed the things keeping me busy, you didn't mention Skyler. All these years, you never really said much about her one way or the other. So I've never really been sure just what you think. About her."

"Hum. The big question. Let's catch a few more fish for breakfast tomorrow. We'll talk while we fish. Here, help your old man get up. Hate to admit it, but I stiffened up a bit after our hike. Come on, grab the rods and let's wake some fish."

Dad got up with a groan while Jake grabbed his fishing gear and the lamp they used to light our cloth house, following him back down to the water. As they set up, Dad began again to speak.

"Okay, so what can I say about Skyler? She sure is pretty, and she always struck me as quite clever. I guess my thoughts are more about how you feel. Where do you want to go in life, and is she the one you want to go there with?"

"I'm not sure I understand. Is it like the story you told me about the girl you were dating when you met Mom, and you asked yourself whether you'd want her to raise your kids if you couldn't be there? Is that what you mean?"

"Well, yeah, that's a piece of the puzzle, but

there's more. I told you a bit about my time in Vietnam, about my temper, and the trouble I got in. I should have shared more. Maybe it would have helped you understand why I'm so difficult at times. But I don't like talking about some of the things I saw. No sane person who's killed someone or had a friend die as they held their hand, waiting for an evac helicopter, wants to talk about those experiences. I've kept a lot bottled up, which wasn't good for us."

Dad spoke softly, but his words hung in the air like the incoming fog across the water.

"I was angry and lost when I got back. Yeah, I was seeing someone, but it wasn't going anywhere. I was drinking and getting into lots of fights. Then I met your mom. She was different from any women I knew. Intelligent, kind, with a gentle quality to her like nothing I'd ever experienced. All that and still tough as nails. I guess your mother saw something in me too, but she also saw the darkness. And she wasn't going to have it in her life. I told you she set me straight. Her inner strength and goodness made me want to be a better person. She told me she cared for me, but she wasn't going to link her life to someone who didn't share her goals. So if I was interested in a future with her, I needed to clean up my act."

Dad sighed and shook his head. "Like I said, tough as nails. You know the rest. I'm still no altar boy, but I got help. I talked to counselors at the VA, helping me deal with what I did and saw. I started going to AA meetings and haven't had a drink in twenty-five years. In those early years, I went to a meeting almost every night, trying to manage my anger. Your mother never complained about time away from her or the baggage I had to work through.

"We're responsible for everything we do in our lives, and I believe I *could* have found my way without your mother by my side. But I'm thankful I didn't have to. So when I think of who you might spend your life with, I hope you find someone who'll be there for you like your mother's been for me. I want you to find someone to push you, challenge you to be everything you can be, and call you out if you aren't true to your own best self. Skyler seems nice enough. Only you can answer whether she is the woman who can be all those things for you."

Jake and Dad stood by the edge of the lake, dragging their sticks through the water as they checked their strings for any sign of a hungry fish. But while Dad talked, it seemed neither of them was thinking about the fish they were supposed to catch. Dad grew silent while Jake stared intently out past the long, flat water. I tried to nuzzle against him, but he didn't notice. So I sat by his side while Jake stared out, looking for something beyond the end of his string trailing along the bottom of the pond on its own lonely quest.

~ ~ ~ ~

The next morning, Jake and Dad set up to fish again, and my ears drooped. I'd hoped we'd head back to more familiar smells, to a place filled with less potential dangers. But my humans wanted to remain, so I squared my shoulders and lifted my nose in the air. I must stay ready, making sure I did my part to keep them safe.

I slept little the next few nights and remained alert for any signs of danger. But no threat came close. Each morning, I'd head off to discover what happened around our camp overnight. I remained amazed by the animals I scented and the various activities that occurred during the night. I found the familiar smells of squirrels and rabbits, along with signs of their most significant threat: coyotes. I also found the droppings of the large cat. Happily, I discovered no fresh signs of the giant beast that had worried me so. Perhaps our appearance caused him to move on. But I remained alert for signs of the large cat or this other unknown giant, bigger than any of us. I sat through each night in the darkness, hoping it would be our last night there. But, regardless of how long we stayed, I'd be prepared to warn my family if danger approached. The fish remained plentiful and delicious, and I loved being with my family, but I was ready to go home.

Finally, after several sleepless nights, Jake and Dad took down our cloth house early one morning. It was time for us to move on. Tired, I needed to sleep through the night without concern for big cats, packs of coyotes, or giant nameless beasts sneaking into our camp.

Moving away from our camp, I thought we were leaving the danger behind, not realizing we were walking directly toward it.

Unwelcome Stranger

The weather changed for our trip back. We woke to an ugly gray morning and hurriedly ate our first cold breakfast in several days. After so many lovely warm days, we now walked down the mountain with a strong wind at our backs. With the wind blowing behind me, I couldn't be sure what was ahead, but I had the strong scent of the large cat who appeared to trail us while we slowly moved away from her home. I was pretty confident a cat, even a very big one like this, wouldn't try to attack our pack. Cats are crafty and usually hunt animals who are alone and vulnerable. The cat was probably keeping a watchful eye on us to make sure we left its hunting area. I slowed my walk, trailing behind Jake and Dad, tracking the cat's movements while it did the same to us.

Up ahead, Jake and Dad kept a steady conversation going while they walked. I've always been amazed at how much humans have to say, but it does seem to please them. I still loved the sound of their voices and was happy to hear them drone on while we hiked down the mountain.

Approaching a sharp turn in the trail, Jake and Dad stopped talking as they moved slowly, concentrating on the narrowing trail. It had begun to rain, and the wind at our backs grew stronger. They stepped cautiously on the slippery path, checking their footing as they hugged the tall rocks on one side, trying to avoid coming close to the slick wet edge and its steep decline. Then, moving along the side of a tall rock wall, they turned, passing out of sight.

"Dad!"

The fur shot up on my back as Jake's voice, frightened and surprised, rang out.

"Jake, don't turn away. Stand straight. Make yourself tall as you can." Dad called out to Jake, his voice firm and commanding.

I raced around the rock wall that hid them from me.

Standing there, within pouncing distance of Jake, was a giant animal up on its back legs. With his front paws raised high in the air, he stared directly at Jake.

How had I let this happen? All the time I had been watchful for the large cat trailing behind us, I never sensed this threat directly ahead in our path. With the rain and wind blowing from behind, I'd remained attentive to the cat's movements and been totally surprised by this menace looming over the boy I loved.

Jake's legs quivered, fighting the urge to turn and run, but My Boy held firm. He righted himself, never standing taller. Somehow he understood, like in most fights, turning and running usually put you at greater risk than facing the challenge head-on.

The giant roared, flashed powerful teeth, and dropped onto its front paws, bolting toward Jake.

I had to act. I lunged forward, throwing myself into the air, knocking myself and the furry black giant to the ground just as it was about to land on Jake. The giant and I came up snarling and growling, each measuring the other. Swiping at me with a huge paw, its sharp claws tore into my side.

I yelped in fiery pain. Stunned and bleeding, I turned again to face the giant while Jake, at least for the moment, scrambled out of danger. The giant focused all its fury on me, standing back on its hind legs again to tower over me. I knew I could not win in a long-drawn-out battle, but I would not allow this deadly beast to get any closer to Jake or Dad.

I had surprised the giant with my initial attack, coming from behind the rocks and knocking it over. I would not be able to surprise it again. And whatever choice I made in the next few moments would be vital for the safety of my family.

I moved slowly across the narrow muddy trail, cautiously circling the beast, knowing a steep fall onto the jagged rocks far below could be my fate if I didn't hold my ground against my powerful foe. Perhaps frightened by Jake's sudden presence when we'd appeared without warning from around the rocks, the giant's instinct had been to attack. But after being knocked over and realizing there were three of us, the beast seemed less sure of its next move.

To show fear or turn away would put all of us at risk. With the fur high on my back, I snarled and shifted, keeping myself between the giant and Jake as my back paws moved dangerously closer to the slippery edge. I didn't know what would happen or what I could do, but I had to protect My Boy.

Off to my side, Dad bellowed like a wild animal. The sound was unlike any I'd ever heard come from a human. Dad had grabbed a long stick from the ground and waved it violently in the air, shouting at the giant. Jake found some safety off to the other side, and he too stood tall, howling. Then Dad and Jake began to call my name, shouting instructions.

But I didn't listen. I had to protect my family. A snarl filled my chest. My side ached, and blood flowed steadily from the wide gash as I continued to circle the looming danger.

Finally, he roared once again, like he had the moment before he'd rushed at Jake.

"Jake! The knapsack behind you. Bear spray in the front flap. Quickly!" Dad shouted out.

In that instant, the beast decided. He dropped down onto his front paws, and in two huge bounds, he was on top of me.

I'd learned of the speed and power the beast possessed in his front paws from our first flurry. So I evaded the deadly blow from a swiping paw but couldn't avoid the weight of his body. We collided with a painful thud, and I tumbled to the ground with the giant landing on top of me. I spun out from under him, quickly maneuvering to get on top of him. I buried my teeth into his throat, and the taste of warm blood filled my mouth. He swiped again and again at me with his mighty paws. But I was too close for him to have great power with the blows. I wasn't strong enough to maintain this hold against such strength for more than a few moments, but I would fight as long as I could to keep him from my family. Then, with a chilling roar, the giant broke free and fell on me again with a blinding heaviness. His enormous mouth closed over my head as his deadly jaw tightened on me.

I had lost.

Helpless to escape the slow crushing power of his bite, all strength left my body. My last thoughts were hoping I'd somehow created enough time for Jake and Dad to find safety.

Then, strangely, the beast released me from his death grip, deafeningly crying out in tremendous pain. He stood tall on his back legs, towering over me, and roared once more before turning to run off. Only then did I notice the air filled with a terrible smell. My eyes burned, and I struggled to breathe. I couldn't tell what felt worse, this new choking sensation or the pain from my battle with the giant.

I stood up and staggered over to Jake. He was on his knees crying, his shoulders hunched, holding a can in his hand.

He was safe. That's all I needed to know. I dropped to the ground at his feet, and despite the burning in my eyes, I closed them and went to a place I'd never been before.

Off the Mountain

"**D**ad, is he . . . ?"

"He's still breathing, but the bear mauled him badly. Quick, get the first aid kit from the knapsack. Gotta bind these wounds and fast."

Dad knelt over me, wiping away the blood, and ran his strong hands across my entire body. He lingered a long time at my shoulder and side, where the giant had slashed me with the first swipe from his huge paw. Then Dad softly touched my face and head, washing away the blood, running water over my eyes, all the while whispering my name and telling me what a good boy I was. I tried to move but couldn't and closed my eyes again.

My family was safe.

"He sacrificed himself for me." Jake's voice was breathless and raw.

"No time for that. Help me get some disinfectant in these wounds. We can't let any of this start to fester. We need to clean and bind them best we can and get Bull off this mountain. We'll cut a couple of saplings to improvise a stretcher and camp at the bottom of this ridge tonight. Come morning, we'll carry him out."

That night, I didn't keep watch through the darkness. Jake tried to feed me some of the salty meat they carried in their pack, but I wasn't hungry. He put water into a bowl for me to drink, but I couldn't lift my head. Finally, Dad poured water into Jake's cupped hand, and I slowly licked his fingers to cool my burning throat. I fell asleep, not waking until the first glimmer of light appeared in the morning sky.

Jake and Dad had already packed up our camp, ready to go. I couldn't get up, feeling an ache throughout my body and more tired than I ever remembered. I just lay there. I yelped, and my paws jerked when they lifted me onto a piece of cloth attached to poles. Then they bent over, grabbed the poles, and turned from camp, heading down the mountain.

I slept again. I'd wake through the morning to feel the sun on my face, the bad weather of the day before now gone. I heard faint sounds, but unlike other trips, Dad and Jake had little to say. Instead, the sound of pounding feet and their heaving breathing carried me back to sleep each time I woke.

"Tired?"

"No. Gotta get him to a vet. How's he look?"

"About the same, but we're getting close. Just a few more miles."

My eyes opened. I don't know how long I'd slept, but the sun hung higher in the sky. I heard quickened footsteps and heavy breathing. Then Jake and Dad were yelling.

"Here! Over here! Over here!"

I smelled the smoke from a car and struggled to

lift my head. A man in a brown uniform jumped out of a big truck and ran toward us, and I dropped my head to sleep once more.

I woke to an unfamiliar voice.

"This is one incredibly lucky dog, but he's taken a tremendous beating. The gash across his shoulder and ribcage was real nasty. You did a good job binding it. Miracle he didn't bleed out . . . Took close to a hundred stitches . . . Half his ear is gone with very deep punctures on his head and snout from when the bear's jaw locked on him. One puncture is directly above his right eye. An inch lower, and the tooth could have cut right through the soft eye tissue to his brain and killed him on the spot. You got to the bear spray just in time. A moment or two longer, and his skull would have been crushed.

"He's stirring. Sedative's wearing off. He'll be in a lot of pain but should be fine, barring infection. I bombarded him with antibiotics. You two saved his life, getting him off that mountain so quickly."

"He risked his life for us."

I opened my eyes to the sound of Dad's familiar voice, but a woman hovered over me. She had a tender touch and self-assurance in every move she made. She looked intently at me, her hands moving swiftly across my aching body, pausing for a moment to touch my face.

Bright lights surrounded me. How long had I slept? I struggled to remember. Where was My Boy? Panicked, I raised my head high, searching.

Jake stood right behind the woman. Dad had his arm around Jake's shoulder, holding him up. Their faces streaked with dirt, they both smiled widely as

I lifted my head higher to look at them.

Then, lowering my head, darkness overtook me, and I slept again.

My Boy was safe.

~ ~ ~ ~

"I'm taking Bull to the vet's after work to get his stitches out. You interested?" Dad called to Jake while I rested, warming myself by the sunny window in the front of our house.

"I'm in."

"And while I'm gone, see if you can stop your mother from feeding him. He's getting fat."

Mom came over and hugged me, careful not to touch any place that might cause a yelp or whimper.

"Good luck with that. Don't you read the local papers? This dog's a hero. Risked his life to save my son and husband from a deadly bear attack. I'll be cooking steak for him till he's lost interest."

"With Bull's appetite, that might take quite a while, Mom."

I was feeling stronger every day. Lots of visitors came to our house to see me. Some people I knew, like Maria and her family, plus Sam and Dougie, but several strangers came to visit too. I could tell they were all talking about me because they said my name a lot. Jake or Mom always sat by my side, petting me and saying I was a good boy. And my tail beat against the floor whenever Jake called me by my favorite name of all: Best Boy.

One night, a fancy lady with paint around her eyes came to visit. A big man with a furry face came with her. He set up bright lights that lit the room like outside in the middle of the day. The lady sat and talked to my family, and they called me over to sit by her side, even though it got really hot near those lights. I stayed but kept hoping they'd leave. I wanted to sit on the cool floor in the room where my family ate and look for any food Mom might accidentally have dropped while she cooked.

I enjoyed the visitors coming to pet me, although they had to be careful around my ear and when scratching my shoulder or belly, not to touch where I'd been injured. But, mostly, it was just good to be with my family and know everyone was safe. I'd relax when the visitors left and my family could be alone.

The days passed, and we saw fewer visitors as our lives returned to normal.

Acceptance Letter

"Well, it's happened. Jake's acceptance letter from the Air Force Academy is on the kitchen table. But now he says he's considering Dartmouth." Mom met Dad at the front door, her voice lacking its usual calm.

"Dartmouth? Let me guess. Skyler applied to Dartmouth. Did she get accepted?"

"She's a legacy."

"Of course, I forgot. No junior colleges or state schools in the pedigree of the Winship family tree. For generations, the kids on the Hill have ended up at Dartmouth or Amherst."

"John, now's not the time,"

"You're right, but what's this about *Dartmouth*? I didn't even know he applied. Jake's wanted to fly since he saw his first airplane, and he set his sights on the Air Force Academy when he was eight and we took him to see the Blue Angels at Hanscom Field. What's happened? Never mind, I know. . . . Skyler happened."

I followed Dad, walking deeper into the house, the anxiousness in his voice matching Mom's, and my tail drooped.

"So, what's he going to do?" Dad asked.

"I don't know. He stormed out when I tried to talk to him. I think he's really torn."

"I blame the girl." Dad's voice grew louder.

"John, that's not fair. Jake's eighteen and is responsible for the choices he makes. We can't blame anyone else. But honestly, I don't think you've ever given Skyler a fair chance."

"Honey, I try. I do. I just can't help it. I've never said a negative word to Jake, but it's been more than three years, and I can't warm to the girl. I know all parents think their kids are special, but God as my witness, there's something rare in Jake. There's goodness, a strength of purpose, and he deserves someone just as special. I just don't see it in that girl, and now she's got him questioning something that's been his dream his entire life." Dad picked up a piece of paper from the table, stared at it, and shook his head. "Dartmouth? You know, he asked me the last time we went camping why I never talked about Skyler."

"Hum. That was a first, and you're just getting around to telling me about it now?"

"Sorry, it was the night before Bull saved us from the bear. When we got back, things were so crazy we never did get a chance to talk."

Mom reached across the table and took away the paper Dad was staring at. "Okay. So please tell me now."

"Well, I wanted to be careful. I didn't want to say something that would be hurtful, but I wanted to give Jake something to think about. Do you remember Carol?"

"Carol, um, the woman you were dating when you met me? Yes, I seem to recall the name."

"Point taken." Dad shrugged, almost like a little boy, and reached out to take Mom's hand. "Okay, well, you know we were kind of serious. At least, that's what we thought. But from the day I met you, I knew you were different. I could tell you had something special."

"Thank you. Now, before I burst, what did you tell Jake when he asked you about Skyler?"

"We talked about Vietnam."

"Really?"

"Yes, we have a few times."

"Wow, well, that makes two people." Mom shifted in her chair, leaning forward, waiting.

"Yes, outside of meetings, you're the only other person I've spoken to about it. But for years, I've known I needed to share with Jake. I'm not proud of how I've handled some things as he's gotten older. I've lost my temper and been pretty hard on him at times. But I wanted him to understand the world I came from and what made me who I am. I hoped talking about what happened over there and then here when I got back might help."

"I'm pleased. I'd hoped you'd open up. John, you don't recognize how strong a presence you are and how your intensity affects people. I've watched Jake as he's gotten older. It's been hard. You fill a room, even while trying not to."

"I know. You've helped me understand things about myself and how it affected Jake. That's why I opened up when he asked me about Skyler. I decided to share some things about our relationship and hoped it would give him some things to think about."

Dad hesitated, slowly shaking his head, his voice growing soft. "We talked about how lost I was when I came back and about meeting you. You were something, going to school and working forty hours a week, emptying bed pans and changing sheets in a nursing home. I saw how you treated those people, the lonely ones, the angry ones, the ones so confused they didn't know where they were. A nineteen-year-old kid, just a little bit of a thing, but you had strength and dignity that made everyone around you better simply by being in your life." Dad stopped and stared at Mom for a long time.

"I told Jake something I never shared with you. I hoped it might resonate with him. But based on this Dartmouth news, I may have wasted my breath."

Mom reached across the table and touched Dad's hand. "He listens, hon, even when you think he isn't. Now, what's your big secret?"

"It happened right after we started working together at the nursing home. I was with Carol one night, talking about having a family, and she said: 'When someone marries, they should be able to look at their partner and tell themselves that's the person I'd want to raise my kid if I couldn't be there.' I agreed. Then I told myself: *And she's not the one*. I explained to Jake what you've meant to me through the years and how I wanted nothing less for him than what I have with you."

Dad stopped and looked at Mom, waiting.

"John DiSpirito, for a hard man, you can say the sweetest things. Now, as for Jake, we have to let go. I hope he doesn't give up on his dreams, but if he does, we'll be there for him as he builds new dreams or picks up the pieces from a mistake."

Dad leaned toward Mom and kissed her, his eyes wet. "I do love you, and you've always seen things I couldn't. I only hope you're right this time too."

My eyes fluttered, sleep calling to me while Mom and Dad walked hand in hand to the room where they slept. The door closed, and I was left behind. I moved to a sunny spot by the window, circled a few times, and dropped to the floor to take my nap. This day they stayed in that room for a long time. Mom came out giggling, and Dad threw himself on the ground to wrestle with me. Mom cooked steaks and made one just for me.

I missed Jake not being around all the time, like when we were younger, but having steak with Mom and Dad was awfully nice. Still, I worried. Would Jake come back to us, or would Skyler continue to pull him farther away from the people who loved him? Mom and Dad mentioned Jake's name a lot while we ate. They were worried too. Like me, they knew he was special, and we had to believe that would help him find his way back home.

Skyler's Lake

Jake stood on the bouncing board, his shirt off, his body already beginning to brown after a long, cold winter. He waived my favorite chew toy back and forth before throwing it into Skyler's lake, shouting for me.

"Go, Bull!"

You didn't have to tell me more than once. I ran hard and jumped, flying in the air, my good ear flopping in the wind. I hit the water with a splash and came up, my paws pumping as I glided through the water, quickly capturing the toy. Holding it softly in my mouth, I turned and swam to the far end of the lake, which amazingly had steps, allowing me to walk out and race back to Jake. I dropped it at his feet and gave myself a quick shake. Jake exploded in laughter while Skyler shrieked her displeasure.

I couldn't understand why Skyler chose to live in a house with its very own lake when she always seemed so worried about getting wet.

Head held high, I barked, signaling I was ready to do it all again. I waited for Jake to throw the toy once more and thought of how I loved chasing the large birds at the lakes in the woods. Somehow, this game we played and my joy at chasing the birds felt connected, but the thought was fleeting. Jake's joyous shouts of "Good Boy" kept me racing into the water over and over while Skyler's groans of displeasure grew louder. With my fur dripping wet, I continued to drop the toy at my best friend's feet.

It was strange, Skyler having her own small lake in the back of her house. It had the board and a slippery slide people climbed up to ride down into the water. It wasn't like any lake I'd ever seen, but lots of things about Skyler's house were different. First, the smells, or the lack of them. It seemed like no one lived here. There were no lingering aromas of food: No hint of a dog or any kind of pet. I could scent the recent presence of Skyler, her mother, and the woman they called Carlotta, but I never saw Carlotta out near the lake. She spent all her time in the house, running a cloth over the furniture or pushing that noisy machine across the fluffy carpets. If the house smelled of anything, it was the liquid Carlotta rubbed into the counters. Its sharp smell burned my eyes and nose when I sniffed too hard.

The house didn't smell like a happy place. Maybe that's why Skyler never seemed happy. She laughed and smiled when people were nearby, but there was never real delight in the laughter. And when Skyler thought no one was watching, she'd closely study others while they laughed and played, as if she were trying to absorb something foreign to her. Maybe because Skyler had to live in this big, lonely house so empty of joy, she never could find any real joy for herself.

This day, Skyler and Jake fell asleep in the hot sun. I sat on the stairs in the low end of the lake, enjoying the cool water. My stomach rumbled. The rumble meant only one thing, time to find some food. Earlier, I'd noticed the door hadn't totally closed when Skyler came out of the house carrying drinks. So I got out of the water, gave myself a quick shake, and walked toward the house. I wasn't supposed to go inside, but I was hungry and wanted to explore. A big house like that had to have food somewhere.

I nudged the door open with my snout and padded inside, my nose twitching, but I could discover no exciting signs. Nothing I sniffed even seemed used, and there was no hint of food. The couches and chairs, the spot on the rug in front of the big screen with the flickering lights where Jake often sat at home eating snacks, all smelled like people were never there. How different Skyler's house was from ours, where every corner and piece of furniture carried the scent of being lived in and loved. The wonderful aromas of cooking and the lives of the people who meant everything to me filled our home. I was glad we lived where we did, even if we didn't have a small lake in our yard for me to play in.

I heard Carlotta upstairs with that noisy machine, so I freely searched the house. Then a familiar shriek pricked my ears.

"Jake, your dog's in the house! Carlotta left a door open, and he's tracked prints throughout the entire first floor and across the new wall-to-wall

Berber carpet in the great room. Carlotta! You need to clean up this mess before you go home. My mother will have a fit. Jake, you know my mother doesn't want that dog in the house."

"I'm sorry, Miss Skyler. I didn't realize. You were all by the pool when I went upstairs to clean."

"Bull, come over here, buddy." Jake leaned forward, slapping his hands on his thighs and calling me. "Now, look what you've done. You've gotten Carlotta and me in trouble with the mistress of the house. Carlotta, I'll grab another mop and help you clean up."

"Oh no, Mr. Jake. I couldn't let you do that."

"Of course, you can. My dog made the mess. It's only right I help clean up, and please, it's Jake. I feel uncomfortable when you call me *Mr.* Jake."

Jake grabbed a towel and got down on his knees, wiping up paw prints from the floor.

"Jake, what are you doing? We were going to go to the movies, and now you're volunteering to do our housekeeper's job?"

"Skyler, please. I'm not going to go to the movies and leave someone else to clean up a mess I'm responsible for." Jake's voice was calm but firm, like when he'd tell Dougie he planned to finish one of his books instead of playing one of Dougie's crazy games.

"Oh, here we go again. Mr. Egalitarian a friend of the common people. Some may admire your noble senses, but it's a bit too much. We'll be at Dartmouth in the fall, and you're working for my father now, not cutting lawns. You're going to be very successful in life. You better get used to being rich and letting people do things for you. You'll find you're treated differently because you have money, and you have to learn how to handle people."

"I don't know about any of that, but today I'm helping Carlotta clean up the mess Bull made. And about Dartmouth, you told everyone at school about my acceptance letter. I just got wrapped up in the excitement of it all. Now I'm not so sure."

"Jake, you can't turn your back on the type of opportunities Dartmouth would provide And we both agreed this way, we could be together every day."

"I know, and my parents insisted they'd make it work financially, but they don't have that kind of money." Jake had been happy and joking, helping Carlotta, but turning to face Skyler, he grew serious. "They've saved for years, but they weren't planning on an Ivy League tuition. I saw the look in their eyes when we got the financial aid packet and started doing the math. Besides, you know I always wanted to fly. It may seem corny to some people, but I think there's something special about serving your country. They'd never say it to me, but my parents think I've given up on my dream."

"Not that again. Now is not the time for this conversation." Skyler's usually cool eyes flashed hot, and she spun away, heading back out to her lake.

Jake had scolded me in front of Skyler, but his face wore a crooked smile. His tone and the look in his eyes showed me he wasn't truly mad. He nudged me with his hip, sending me out in the sun to dry off while he stayed inside working with Carlotta, wiping that towel across the wet floors.

Skyler, sitting in the sun, paid no attention to me. I thought of the first time I'd met her. She'd dropped to the ground with that squeal of hers, acting excited to see me while Jake stood by watching with his broad smile. But something was missing. As time passed, I noticed Skyler only acted interested in me when Jake was nearby and ignored me when he wasn't.

In all the time I'd known her, Skyler never found my favorite spots to pet or scratch. She never scratched behind my ears or the spot high up on my chest that set my back paw to thumping. My friends ran their fingers back and forth quickly across that spot or gave me the belly rubs they all knew I liked so much. For Skyler, if Jake wasn't around, it was like I wasn't there either.

But that was all right with me. In many ways, dogs are smarter than people. We figure out pretty quickly who is truly interested in being our friend and who isn't. And we don't bother with those people who aren't interested in us.

The fact Skyler didn't want to be my friend and only acted attentive when Jake was around didn't make me mad. Lots of people enjoyed my company. Jake, Mom, Dad, Maria, and her brothers all loved me and wanted to be with me all the time. I just couldn't figure out why Jake was so interested in being around Skyler.

Sure, she had a lake in her backyard and a car without a top, which was wonderful to ride in. I guess she was kind of pretty, in a human sort of way, but there wasn't much more to Skyler than that. At least not anything I could find. She lacked the kindness I sensed in Jake the first day we met. She didn't have the strength I saw in Mom and Dad, or the sense of loyalty Maria showed, or the joy for life Dougie had, or the simple goodness I saw in Diego. Skyler didn't show any of these qualities, but Jake clearly cared for her, so I would always be polite around her. Maybe there was something I didn't see, something she was afraid for others to see.

Or maybe, in time, Jake would realize there wasn't anything special enough about her. Jake was smart and kind. Whatever the truth, Jake would know when he finally saw it.

For now, I relaxed, drying off in the warm sun while Skyler vigorously scraped her nails with the thin brown stick she always kept in her bag. I heard her talking, but the words were not meant for me. So I dozed lazily.

"Sometimes, he makes me want to scream. Always talking about *doing the right thing*. Still, this talk of going to the Air Force Academy or his silly dreams about becoming a writer. He can be so naïve, but I will bring him around. You better believe I will."

Maria's Plans

I lay at Maria's feet. She'd come by earlier with Diego to take me on a long walk. When we got back, Mom gave Diego something to eat before he went home, leaving Maria to visit Mom and me.

With her muddy shoes left outside on our stairs, Maria ran her feet across my back while taking small nibbles on a treat and talking to Mom. Dogs can tell when people really care and want to be with us, and knowing this makes us love and want to be with them. With Maria's feet gently resting on me, I was with people who loved me, so I slumbered contentedly. There was nowhere else I'd rather be. Relaxed and happy, I still stayed attentive in case any of her food crumbled and fell to the floor.

"I've been talking to my dad about college options and decided next year I'm only applying to local junior colleges. We can save a lot of money, and I can stay home to help with Diego and the twins. I've been thinking about it a lot, and the college experience is overrated. What I'm after is a good education." Maria shifted in her chair and sighed. "Dad didn't want to hear it. He started talking again about escaping Cuba, coming to America as a kid, and all the dreams he has for his children. I'm not trying to be noble. I'm not. I'm just realistic."

Mom usually sat and listened to Maria talk and talk. Never interrupting, she'd smile and nod encouragingly. But not today. Something Maria said caused Mom to straighten in her chair. She interrupted Maria, using her *I've something to say* voice. Like the rest of the family, Maria recognized Mom's tone and fell silent.

"Honey, what are we going to do with you? You know your mother's story. An LPN when she married, she took night classes for years to become an RN. Her dreams were finally coming together when she got sick, and you staying home to play house mom to your brothers isn't part of that dream. Diego is nineteen now. There are adult programs and nearby housing we can investigate for him. Your family's done wonderfully with Diego. He's ready. A moderately self-sufficient life with a part-time job is within his reach. I spoke to Mr. Pham at the corner grocery. Since Binh started at Tufts, they're looking for help stocking shelves and helping the older people carry bags to their cars. Diego could be perfect.

"Maria, you're still a sophomore. The twins will be nearly teenagers when you head off to college. They're good boys and ready for additional responsibilities. There's a beautiful world waiting for you. It's time you reach out and embrace it." Mom paused, her voice softening, but it still had her *you better listen* tone.

"Folks in the Flats aren't rich, but we stick together. If your dad needs anything, we'll be here. So, you, young lady, are going to the school of your choice, and it's not up for debate. It is going to happen."

"You've already spoken to Mr. Pham?" Whatever Mom said had gotten Maria's attention.

"Yes. We can walk down there with Diego Saturday morning and–"

My tail thumped at the sound of the car announcing Jake's arrival. I jumped up and barked, running back and forth from the front window to the door.

"Looks like Jake's home." Mom turned to look out the window as she spoke. "Bull only goes crazy like that for him."

The door opened, and I pounced on Jake, grabbing his sleeve in my mouth and pulling him to the ground to wrestle like we did when we were younger.

"Okay, buddy, can't play right now. Got a date. Oh, hi, Maria, Mom can't stay. Skyler's got this thing at the country club, and I'm already late."

Without waiting for Mom or Maria to speak, Jake rushed past us, closing the door to his room.

"Thanks for the pep talk," Maria said, "and thanks for always being there. Let me take Bull out for a quick run. I know Mr. D has a late shift, and I hate to think of Bull not getting his nighttime walk. Tell Jake, tell him . . . I said bye."

Maria grew silent and snatched my leash. Usually, Maria and Mom could talk for hours, laughing, sometimes crying, but today, with Jake's arrival, Maria was in a sudden rush to leave. Out the door in a flash, Maria's legs churned as we flew up the street, past the houses and shops with their wonderful smells. My paws barely touched the ground, racing across the street and into the park. We didn't stop when we entered. We ran, on and on, until we dropped to the ground under the afternoon shadows of the tall trees, exhausted. With my sides aching, I lay next to Maria, panting.

Maria was upset and still tense, despite our long run. Maybe she missed Jake like I did. But if so, why did we run off as soon as he came back? Was Jake behind Maria's sadness? I nuzzled against her while she, too, struggled for air. She shifted to hug me, her thin brown arms wrapped around my neck, but her sadness lingered as the shadowed sky turned dark.

~ ~ ~ ~

"That poor girl is still crazy about him."

Jake was away with Skyler or at that workplace, and Maria had just left after taking me for another long run. Mom and Dad sat next to each other on the couch, talking while Mom rested her head on Dad's shoulder. I sat at their feet, my head in Mom's lap as she gently scratched under my chin.

Dad sighed. "Yes, and he's completely oblivious. Of course, all parents think no one's good enough for their kids, but I tell you, Jake would be damn lucky to get a girl like Maria. I keep waiting for some light switch to flip on, but he's still fixated on that girl from the Hill and her country-club world. Sometimes, I wonder. Maria's nearly two years younger than Jake, but she seems years older."

"John, we've been here before. Parents can't choose who their kids fall in love with, but I have confidence in Jake. Sure, Maria's younger, but girls mature faster, and Maria had to grow up early, far too early. Jake's eighteen and a bit awed by life outside our working-class side of town. But we've raised him right. If Skyler's the one for him, then there's more there than we see. If there isn't more, well, I trust Jake will see that for himself. In time."

"From your lips to God's ears. I just hope Jake figures out what matters before it's too late. Girls like Maria don't come by every day. I've only met one other in my life, and I married her."

"Yet again, *mi amore*, proof how charming and wise you are." Mom smiled. "I'm sure some of his father's wisdom has rubbed off."

Smiling, Mom and Dad held hands and got up to walk into the room where they slept, leaving me alone. The couch they'd sat on was still warm and filled with their wonderful scent. I hopped up to take a nap, enjoying their closeness, and rested so I would be ready to play when they came back out.

I had steak again that night, but I still missed My Boy.

Part IV

Bad Dreams

I woke with a jolt. Something was terribly wrong. I didn't know why, but an inexplicable fear left me trembling. Ignoring my water bowl and the treat Dad left for me, I panted as I stalked the rooms of the silent house. Something had happened, and I felt powerless to help. What was wrong? Was there anything I could do?

Jake, Dad, and Mom had left our house early that morning. There'd be no long walk or car ride for me. They'd dressed in the clothes they wore when they went to the church place. I didn't get to go there, but I didn't mind. They always came back happy and relaxed, with lots of time for me. So I followed them to the door to say goodbye and then went to lie in my favorite spot by the front window. I'd be there when their car pulled back up in front of the house.

I'd fallen into a fitful sleep but woke, my twitching legs running from an ugly danger I couldn't see. My body shuddered, the scary images leaving me frightened and confused. If Jake were nearby, he'd touch me with his gentle hands and tell me everything was okay. I was only dreaming. But Jake wasn't by my side. So I lay there alone, trembling and thinking of these things Jake called dreams. Disjointed, ugly images of my family, the people I loved, hurt, bleeding, crying out for help, filled my mind, and I couldn't get to them.

Anxiously checking for cars, I raced to the window and looked out to the street, then to the front door, where I could best smell the outside. Nothing. I rushed to the back door, where they sometimes entered the house. But no matter where I looked or sniffed, I could find no sign my family was near.

Dogs don't think about time the way humans do. When our families go out, we don't fret or think, *Where did they go? How much longer will it be?* We know we are loved, and our family will be back soon. It's only a dog with a bad family, made to feel unloved, who will bark nonstop or tear up the house. Usually, when my family went out, I'd take a quick walk around the house to make sure everything was safe and then pick out one of my favorite spots before plopping down for a nice rest. If I woke and they still weren't back, I'd take another short walk inside the house to get a drink of water from my bowl before picking another spot to continue my nap.

But today was different. My frightening dream had changed everything.

There was no chance I'd fall back to sleep. I paced from one spot to the next, looking out the windows, sniffing under doors, and waiting for any sign of my family. But I could find no trace of them.

Trembling, I waited.

The sun moved across the sky while I paced from room to room. I was alone for a long time, much longer than ever before. The house now sat in total darkness, my water bowl dryer than my hanging tongue. If I were younger, I most certainly would have had an accident, but I was too nervous to realize the entire day had passed without going out to do my business.

I panted heavily, my fear growing when at last, my nose twitched at the hint of a familiar scent. My ears perked to the sound of footsteps falling heavily on the walk. The door rattled, then opened, and through the darkness, I saw her. Maria stood in front of me. Her head hung low, unwilling to look at me.

Finally, she reached down, wrapped her arms around my neck, and knelt beside me. I shuddered at the sound of Maria's heartbreaking, pain-filled sobs while she held me tight, her gasps for air vibrating against my body.

Maria's tears told me more than any human words ever could. I didn't know who. Maybe all of them. But a part of my family had been taken from me.

I pulled away from her embrace, spread my legs wide, and with my head held high, surrendered to my pain. My long, sorrowful howls filled the night's darkness, howls telling the world of the loss I felt, the loss I would feel forever.

Maria knelt by my side, her head resting on my shoulders, her hand gently stroking my chest, but the unrelenting pain flowed on. I appreciated her presence, but my heartache was unbearable. So my aching wails continued while Maria, with her arms wrapped around me, waited, understanding nothing she did could make me stop until I was too exhausted to go on.

When I finished, Maria clipped on my leash, gave me a gentle tug, and we stepped from the house into the night. With my tail between my legs, I trailed behind Maria. I stopped next to a tree to do my business but had no interest in sniffing for the tree's information or the stories the cool night air had to share. Instead, I followed Maria to her house, my nose never twitching. I'd been there so many times with Mom or Jake, and her home was always a happy place. I loved playing with the twins and Diego, and everyone was always excited to see me. Diego could stay by my side for hours, gently petting me while their father sometimes scolded the twins not to play so rough as we raced through the house.

This visit was different. I had no desire to play or even rest by someone's side to be petted. Maria's family seemed to understand and respected my feelings, leaving me alone with my heartache and fear. I moped around the house, looking out the window at the street, hoping for any sign of my family. For a dog who usually found waiting quite natural, this was unbearable. I stared out their front window, into the street, for a sign of what was to be.

Finally, late at night, my food untouched, Diego took me to the room he shared with his brothers. Their dad didn't scold him when Diego called me up onto his narrow bed. Deep in the muted darkness, exhausted, I fell asleep with Diego's arms wrapped around my neck.

I spent the next day at Maria's house, again ignoring the fresh food they put out for me, this time sprinkled with bits of cooked meat. I drank a little water and went outside but turned around immediately after doing my business. Maria tugged my leash, trying to convince me to go for a long walk, but I wouldn't follow. I had to stay nearby in case my family came looking for me. I tried to drag her to my home, but my nose told me my family had not returned. So, with my tail between my legs, I trailed Maria back to her house.

I stayed at Maria's house the next few nights, each one much like the last. Sam and Dougie came by one afternoon to visit and talked in hushed voices with Maria. We went for a walk, and I hoped we'd at last end at my house. But with still no scent of my family, we turned away.

Was this to be my life, my family gone forever? I did love Maria almost as much as I loved Mom and Dad. Her family was kind to me, and it was nice to know Dougie and Sam were thinking of me. But they weren't my family. And nothing could repair the empty feeling the disappearance of My Boy had created. I paced the rooms of Maria's small house, my constant panting the only sound in the typically noisy, joy-filled place.

What was to become of me?

Painful Loss

Then, one morning, with the familiar energy back in her step, Maria knelt over me, smiling as she attached my leash. Instead of going for a walk, she signaled me to get in the car, where her father waited. I loved riding in a car, exposed to all the smells, but not that day. I had no interest in anything that took me farther away from the house I shared with Jake and my family. But Maria offered her bright smile and repeated her signal, so, reluctantly, I jumped into the car. Maria sat next to me and rolled the window down, encouraging me to look out, sniff, and enjoy, but I didn't stir. Finally, she gave up and let me ride with my head in her lap while she scratched the nub of my once-wounded ear. We rode on in silence, the only sound the whooshing of the wind through the open window.

We traveled for a long time with lots of stops, starts, and beeping horns. Why were they taking me so far from my home, so far from my family? Outside the window, tall houses, taller than any I'd ever seen, reached into the sky. When we stopped, at last, the car sat in the shadows of one of the tallest ones. Maria got out, and her father leaned forward to speak, touching her hand for a moment.

"Okay, *mi corazón,* there's the entrance to Mass General on the left. I'm going to look for some street parking and will meet you upstairs in a couple of minutes."

Maria tugged at my leash, and I followed her out of the car. But why did we come here? What could possibly be here for me? The house was very big with many, many windows. There were lots of people. Some were pushed in chairs with wheels on them. And there were smells everywhere, all kinds. First came the smells from the street, with all its nearby cars, but then, moving closer to the glass front doors, something else. I smelled sickness, all kinds of sickness. And fear.

Dad often called me a brave dog. I never yelped or whimpered on those warm summer nights when the sky lit up with fire and loud noises hurt my ears. I'd lie in the grass with my family as they oohed and aahed while I ignored all the noises around me. Nearby other dogs might whine and cower, but not me. I was okay. I didn't like the noise, but I was happy with my family by my side.

But my family wasn't with me now, so lonely and frightened, I walked toward this big house with its noises and smell of sickness. With my body quivering and my tail curled tight between my legs, I didn't feel brave at all. Then I could go no farther. I stiffened and pulled back on my leash as I sat down, my shoulders squared. Looking at Maria, I began to shake. Why did she want to bring me to this sad, sad place?

"Bull, please, I know this all very strange to you, but it's important."

I didn't want to go. I couldn't go. Maria could do nothing to make me move toward this terrible place with its awful smell of sickness.

Then a breeze caressed my face. A different scent rushed toward me. Something else. Something familiar and loving.

I looked up, a woof of joy building in my throat. Standing in front of the doors of the giant house was Mom. She stepped toward me, moving slowly, shaky and tired, her arm wrapped in cloth. Her face was marked, as if she'd been in a terrible fight. But there she was, my wonderful, loving Mom.

My tail thumped back and forth along the ground. Breaking from Maria's grasp, I galloped to Mom's side. I wanted to jump on her, wrestle Mom to the ground and smother her with licks, but I could tell I had to be gentle. I stopped and lay down on my back in front of her, my paws outstretched and my tail flopping wildly. I wriggled, trying to be patient while she struggled to lower herself to the ground before hugging me fiercely with her unwrapped arm. Mom kept repeating my name, somehow laughing and crying at the same time. I continued to wiggle under her touch while I licked her tears away till none were left, replaced by the sound of her joyful laughter.

"Thanks for bringing Bull and watching him all this time."

"Please, after everything you and your hus . . . umm . . . family have done for us. We could never pay you back. How's . . . he doing?"

"Who knows. Doctors. Getting a straight answer is like traveling through Dante's circles of hell. He's off the critical list and breathing independently. But there is no sign when . . . or if. Sorry, this is no time for tears. They aren't saying when he could come out of the coma. It could be days or . . ."

Mom looked small, frail, and frightened in a way I'd never seen. She looked worse than when I first came to live with my family, and she was so wounded. My ear drooped, and I panted, trying to nuzzle closer while she struggled to speak. But just when Mom started to falter, Maria was there to raise her up. She hugged Mom, their bodies melding together like they were one. I cocked my head, surprised to see Maria stood taller than Mom now. Maria looked her in the eye for a moment, hugged Mom again even harder, then whispered something in her ear. I couldn't hear what Maria said, but it brought a broad smile to Mom's face. Maria looked down at me, and her voice grew louder.

"And that's why Bull is here. I still can't believe you convinced the doctors to let us bring him into the hospital, but I should have expected nothing less. I remember Mr. D telling me . . . Sorry."

Mom smiled and touched Maria's face with her good hand. "Honey, it's okay. We only lose loved ones when we stop talking about them. Please, go on."

"Well, it happened one night, you were late with parent-teacher meetings, and I stopped by to walk Bull. I don't remember how, but Mr. D started talking about when Jake was born and you stayed with him in the prenatal ward. He said you wouldn't leave the hospital until Jake could go home with you."

"John told you that?"

"He loved you very much."

"Thank you. People hold so much back, and it's such a waste. They end up filled with remorse for everything they didn't say. We knew how we felt about each other. It was there for all to see." Mom brushed her hand across her wet eyes. "You know John loved you very much too. God never blessed us with a daughter of our own, but we couldn't have asked for a more lovely young woman in our lives.

"I've felt John's presence every day since the accident, and I know nothing would please him more than knowing you were by my side. Now, enough talking. We have work to do."

Mom and Maria were smiling now, all their words somehow helping both of them. Maria put her arm around Mom, gave my leash a gentle flick, and we turned to walk into the giant house. With my family by my side, I was brave enough to enter. My nails clicked as we moved across a cool, slick floor. Doors mysteriously opened as we entered a small room, then just as mysteriously closed behind us. The room shook, and when it stopped, the door opened again, and we were somehow in a different place. The smells grew stronger, sickness, blood, and fear everywhere, but my nose twitched again. I lifted my head as I smelled something else, something wonderful. I shuddered with pleasure at a familiar scent: My Boy.

With my paws skidding across the floor, I dragged Maria into a room where Jake slept in a bed with all kinds of tubes connected to him. I froze, Maria's tight hold on my leash no longer needed. I wanted to run to Jake and shower him with my love, like when I first saw Mom. But something was wrong. Jake wasn't just sleeping. He'd been hurt. Hurt badly. And he was here in this bright room with all the tubes because he needed help to get better. I didn't understand it all, but I knew he'd need me now like never before.

I walked to the bed and placed my head next to his hand. His other hand had tubes attached, but this one was free. I ached for him to touch me, scratch behind my ears or under my chin, or just rest his hand on my head. But he didn't. Perhaps he couldn't. He didn't move at all. So I sat there next to him and fell asleep, my head gently resting against his motionless hand.

I woke to the sound of Maria's voice.

"Okay, Bull, we have to go. We can come back tomorrow."

I loved Maria. She had become part of my family, and I always tried to do whatever she asked of me. But not that day. I leaned back, holding my head high. I straightened my shoulders and pulled back stubbornly while she pulled, trying to force me forward. Nothing Maria or Mom said or did could get me to leave Jake's side.

Finally, looking very sad, Maria's papa came over. He reached out to take the leash from Maria. He gently stroked the side of my face and gave one hard tug on the leash, signaling for me to come. I knew I was stronger even than him, but suddenly, I felt terrible for being a naughty dog. Jake wouldn't want me to act this way. I had to be the best dog I could be for Jake. So I stood up, licked Jake's hand, and with one last look back at the boy I loved, I followed Papa Tomás out of the room and away from the boy who was my life.

Waiting

I went back to our house with Mom. It was good to be in my own home and smell all those familiar aromas, but there were no signs of the joy that typically filled our home. Instead, Mom walked through the door, unclipped my leash, and fell on the couch, forgetting to put water in my bowl. I stayed by her side, listening to her heavy breathing while the house grew dark.

When she woke, Mom gave me water and fed me, never looking at me or speaking. Her sadness was worse than when I first came to live with my family, and I could do nothing to bring that light back into her eyes. I brushed against Mom and put my head in her lap when she began to cry, but her sorrow only grew. Finally, late in the night, Mom called me onto her bed. She wrapped her one good arm around me and, crying, fell into a restless sleep.

Dogs don't cry, and I didn't want to wake Mom by howling, but I wished I could do something to ease my pain. Mom wasn't crying only for Jake, although that would've been enough to make her sob. She wept for Dad.

My bad dream had been true. Whatever happened to scar Mom and injure Jake had hurt Dad worse. He was gone. His smell lingered in the house. I could remember his strong hands petting me, but he was gone from this home forever. Oh, how I wanted to howl. But Mom's slow, unsteady breathing after finally falling asleep was more important than my need to show my pain. I lay awake by her side, sadder than I knew I could be.

The next few days, Mom, Maria, and I took the long drive to that big house to visit Jake. Sam and Dougie came most days as well, and Dougie had never kept this quiet as even he seemed unable to find much to say. Skyler came to visit one day, but she didn't stay long, and she didn't come back again. Mom got a bit stronger each day, but sadness hung over her, a sadness I couldn't help chase away.

In hard times, my family worked together. But now, with only me by her side, Mom and I moved through the sad days alone. And I sat helpless, unable to ease the pain that surrounded us.

When visiting, I'd rest my head next to Jake's hand, hoping to be touched. But he didn't stir. After the first day, no one had to force me to leave. I was a good boy. Jake needed to rest, and I trusted they'd bring me back the next day. Eventually, they moved Jake to a different room, where fewer people came bustling in and out to check on him. But beyond this, nothing changed from one visit to the next.

Finally, one day after a long visit, the boys stood up, ready to leave. Mom didn't have her arm wrapped up any longer. She could drive again, but

Maria still came, along with Dougie and Sam. Mom flicked my leash, signaling time to go, but I didn't respond. My body stiffened. I had to stay.

"Come on, Bull, don't give me that look. We have to go. I'm back at work and need to stock the fridge so I can spend as much time here as possible."

I didn't listen. Mom wanted to go, but I couldn't leave. My Boy needed me at that very moment, and I would not leave him. Something had changed.

I jerked away and put my head back next to Jake. Sam came over to take the leash from Mom, prepared to give it a hard tug, but then it happened.

At first, no one but me noticed. It seemed like the blanket shifted when I'd put my head back on the bed, but it wasn't that. It was more, much more. Ever so slowly, Jake's fingers moved, and he raised his hand, like a leaf caught in a gentle breeze, then let it fall to rest on top of my head.

Mom called out at the unmistakable sign of Jake's gentle touch. "Oh my God, Doctor! Nurse! Someone! His eyelids are fluttering. He moved his hand!"

"Bull..."

It was Jake's voice, strange and weak, but he'd spoken. My Boy had spoken.

"Yes, Jake . . . Bull's here, and Maria. Sam and Dougie too. We've been here every day."

Jake's pale face strained, his eyes traveled around the room, his hand barely moving after coming to rest on my head. But My Boy was touching me. His eyes grew more alert, and he struggled to speak, his voice strained.

"Mom, what happened? What am I doing here?"

"We were in a car accident. You've been in a coma for nearly three weeks. You gave us a heck of a scare."

Other peopled raced into the room while they spoke. A slender man in a long white shirt and a woman now stood beside us. The woman smiled and attended to Jake with quick, confident hands. The man's eyes were open, wide, and alert, but no smile crossed his face. Instead, he gave directions to the smiling lady in a firm voice and walked over to the side of Jake's bed. He asked Jake lots of questions, then asked him to do little things, almost like you do when training a puppy.

"Squeeze my hand. Tight as you can. Good, now with the other hand. Harder. Harder. All right. Can you wiggle the toes on your right foot? Excellent. Now your left. Hum. Try again. A little more, a little more. That's okay. It will come. Close your left eye and follow my finger. Good. Now your other eye. Uh-huh. All right, now, I know you're tired, just a few more questions, and you can rest. What's your name?"

"Jake. Jake DiSpirito."

"How old are you?"

"Ah, um, eighteen."

"Very good. What school do you go to? Jake, can you tell me what school you go to?"

"I . . . I can't remember."

"That's fine, Jake. Just fine. It will come back, in time. Now listen, I want you to relax. The nurse will clean you up and order you a little something to eat. What do you say to some nice broth? You've been on an IV for weeks and lost a lot of weight. We've got to put some meat back on those bones of yours."

While everyone hugged and cried, the man in the long white coat, his face still serious, continued to speak to Jake. But even Sam wouldn't stop grinning while Dougie repeated the same thing to anyone who would listen.

"Told ya. Didn't I tell ya? Didn't I tell ya?"

The man gave the boys a look like Mom did when they broke something in the house, and Maria tugged on my leash, signaling me to follow the noisy boys out of the room.

I hesitated. I didn't want to go, but Jake needed to rest. So I let Maria lead me out of the room, leaving the smiling lady alone with Jake to wash his face and help him drink from a cup.

My Boy was finally awake. He would come home to us.

My tail whooshing, I followed Maria to lie at her feet outside the room. She sat near the food machines where Mom stood with the man in the long shirt while the boys raced around us, whooping and hollering. Dougie rode on Sam's back and waved his arms high in the air, shouting to anyone who would listen.

"I told ya. I told ya. Nothin's gonna beat our man Jake!"

Another lady, not happy, like the one helping Jake, hurried over, scolded the boys, and told them to go outside. Shooed away, the boys disappeared, but not before giving Maria and me big hugs of celebration. Mom, smiling wide for the first time in a long while, watched them leave and turned back to talk to the serious man who had hovered over Jake.

"Your son's a very lucky young man. He had a fifty-fifty chance of making it through the first night, and the next few days were touch and go. After that, there were still serious risks. Comas are a great unknown. His physical condition stabilized enough that we were days away from recommending a transfer to an extended care facility specializing in long-term coma patients. I don't use this word lightly, but it is a small miracle he's where he is today. It's truly amazing."

"Doctor, I sense a *but* coming."

"Well, yes. I'm sorry to say there are some buts, and they could be significant. Jake has experienced severe neurological damage. As you saw, he also displays some pronounced motor impairment on the left side of his body. His memory's impacted, and he has damaged vision in his left eye that may require additional surgery. It's too early to tell how impactful this all may be. We'll have to do a complete series of neurological and physical tests, but I want to prepare you for the reality your son may never be quite the same, physically or mentally. You'd mentioned the Air Force Academy. I don't want to be premature, but I want you to manage your expectations. And Jake's. It would be best to prepare for the real possibility college might not be in Jake's future."

Mom's body tensed, and my tail stopped wagging. Her jaw tightened, and she had a familiar look. Fear? Anger? No, it was strength. The strength she showed when she refused to listen to someone tell her no. Maria noticed the tension and stirred beside me as I sat up. Mom squared her shoulders and grew bigger before my eyes till she looked like the tallest person in the room.

"Thank you, Doctor. You and everyone at the hospital have been wonderful, but you don't know Jake. He's focused, with a work ethic that would silence a Marine drill sergeant. He's never been a typical kid. If a teacher asked for a five-page essay, he'd give ten. If a coach said train for two hours every day, he'd train for four. Can I tell you something about that boy in there?"

"Please." The serious man smiled for the first time that day, and he leaned forward to listen.

"Jake was always on us about getting a dog. Well, with our family's hectic schedule, that was the last thing we needed. But my husband and I had run out of ways to say no."

Mom paused and smiled, like she enjoyed telling her story, and then continued.

"When Jake was beginning junior high, getting him up each day was like waking the dead. It didn't matter what time he went to bed or how much sleep he got, he couldn't get going in the morning. But his school had an excellent program. Kids who came in an hour early to satisfy their PE requirement could take an extra college prep course. We wanted Jake to do this but thought there was no way we'd be able to get him up an hour earlier. So when he started in again about a dog, we told him he could get a puppy if he took the early morning class. We figured we had nothing to lose. If Jake couldn't do it, we'd be off the hook, and if a miracle occurred, we'd be helping him academically.

"Well, he accepted the challenge. He removed all the curtains and shades in his room and bought himself an alarm clock with the most annoying buzzer imaginable. He rearranged his room so the morning light hit his bed and the light switch was right next to him when he woke. For the first three months of junior high, Jake got up, showered, and was out the door thirty minutes earlier than he needed to be. So that December, a week before Christmas, Jake got the best present of his life. He's lying right there next to that pretty girl. His name is Bull. A hundred twenty pounds of loving, loyal energy. He's proof of what my son can accomplish when he sets his mind."

Mom kept saying Jake's name like there was something she needed this man to understand. Then her voice softened, but her face continued shining bright.

"Doctor Yoshida, thank you for your carefully measured words. I know they come from a caring place. But you tell us what we need to do, what therapy is required, what exercises you recommend, and we'll do them twice over. That boy has too much potential. I refuse to believe . . . refuse to accept a half-life with physical and intellectual limitations is what God planned for him. Jake has this miraculous second chance at life, and he will not waste it. I know my son. He won't quit until he's back. He may not have the exact life he planned, but I promise you, Jake will be better for this. And when my son walks on the dais to accept his college diploma, I'd like you to be there."

The man's smile grew, and he reached out to

take Mom's hand.

"Your family's support system has amazed me, and nothing would please me more than to be wrong. Now, the next few weeks will be crucial. First, let's get the test results back and set up a therapy schedule. I can tell you, a positive attitude, a commitment to work till you are bone-tired, and faith in a higher power will hugely benefit Jake's recovery. Mrs. DiSpirito, I'm a person of faith too, and there's a Buddhist quote that's helped me. 'We are what we think. All that we are arises with our thoughts. With our thoughts, we make the world.' I sense you believe that too. I hope Jake can see a complete recovery. But I warn you, he's got a very long, uncertain road ahead."

"Thank you, Doctor. Jake knows we get the life we make for ourselves. I trust him to make the most he can from this second chance."

Mom turned away from the man, a strange look in her eyes. It was the same look Dad had when we battled the giant beast. With her head high and looking straight ahead, Mom walked back into Jake's room, shouting for me to follow.

"Bull, we've got work to do!"

Homecoming

Jake came home tired and weak. He spoke slowly and moved in an odd, shuffling way, but My Boy had come back to me.

Jake woke early every day, and we'd go for walks, at first, very short ones. Then, day by day, they grew longer. In the past, I'd linger, taking time to mark spots so other dogs would know I'd been there. I'd sniff to see if any new dogs had come by, check if any neighborhood dogs might be sick, had pups due, or so many other things dogs learn from smelling the world around us. But things had changed. We had a purpose now, and I followed Jake's shaky lead while he pushed himself forward. If he stopped, so did I, always careful to move at Jake's pace. I didn't dawdle on these walks. Jake needed to get stronger, and it was my job to help him.

In the early days, Jake dragged one leg badly, shuffling like he'd been in a fight, walking much like I did after I battled that giant in the woods. Jake would grit his teeth, struggling to lift his bad leg higher and higher while he walked on, never quitting. Then, ever so slowly, he began to drag it a little less. But our walks were just the start of each very long day.

Jake had made a new friend named Dave, but their time together wasn't always friendly. Dave arrived each day, immediately after we got back from our walk. Like Mom, Dave had two names. Jake also called Dave "Doctor Death." Sometimes, Jake smiled when he called Dave that. But usually, covered in sweat and with his face creased in pain, Jake would shout it out in anger, his voice shaking the house with its power. Dave was big, like Sam, and he looked strong, maybe even stronger than Dad. Like Dad, Dave played all kinds of games with Jake, but the tension in Jake's body and his flashes of temper made it look like these games weren't much fun.

Dave would throw Jake a ball and make him catch it with the hand that hung by his side, the same side as the leg Jake dragged. I'd typically chase any ball I see, but these were special balls for Jake, so I never chewed or chased them, even if they flew past me, tempting me to play.

I'd sit watching while Dave made Jake squeeze the ball till Jake's head dropped in exhaustion, and still, Dave called out, challenging Jake for one more. One more. Sometimes they wrestled, Dave leaning on Jake's bad leg or pushing Jake's bad arm back and forth, causing Jake to call out in pain, but unwilling to quit.

"Is that all you've got, Doctor Death? You're going to have to do better than that. They told me you were the best. They told me you could push me."

They'd only stop for a moment while Jake shouted at Dave, and they'd be back at it, not stopping until Jake fell silent, dripping in sweat. Often Sam and Dougie came and shouted at Jake, cheering him on as he played his games.

"One more! One more! You've got one more. Come on, push. Push, DiSpirito. You've got this!"

After Dave left, Jake would be exhausted and sweating. He'd take a break to clean up, grab something to eat, and be back at it again. Sometimes, Jake played the entire Dave visit games all over again by himself, playing Dave's part as well. And then there'd be more games, like the family used to play, or new games Jake appeared to make up himself. At times, Jake played with one of the boys or with Mom or Maria, but if they weren't around, he played the painful, confusing games by himself.

Skyler came by a few times, but she didn't enjoy the games like Mom or Maria. Skyler would fidget with an uncomfortable smile on her face, seeming impatient with Jake when he didn't play the game well. She didn't join in the enthusiastic cheering like the others did when Jake won.

We started to see less and less of Skyler.

One day, Skyler visited but again left quickly after getting impatient with Jake's games. Without turning to see her go, Jake started up again, pushing even harder than usual. Jake continued on, exhausting himself, playing the games alone more intensely than he ever had with Dave. Then, with sweat dripping from his body and his face wearing his now-familiar scowl, Jake kept repeating angry, strange words.

"I know what you think. I see the pity. You don't need a speech-slurring, gimpy-legged boyfriend holding you back."

Jake was angry a lot after the accident. I'd follow him everywhere he went, brushing against him, trying to make him smile, but we'd lost the happy, gentle boy I loved so much. Jake got impatient over little things that never bothered him before, yelling at his family. He'd become a stranger to us all. Once, while playing one of the games alone, Jake got so upset he threw a plate of food against the wall, shattering it to pieces and frightening me so much I ran from the room with a yelp. The door slammed behind me, followed by the sounds of Jake grunting as he went back to playing his anger-filled, painful games.

I stood outside the room, shut off from My Boy, unable to help. I paced back and forth, returning to scratch at the door, but it wouldn't open, Jake's heavy breathing drowning out the sound of my paws beating against the door. Finally, exhausted, I dropped to the ground and waited, listening to the sound of Jake's groans, pushing himself harder to win this game that had become so important to him.

When the door opened, Jake's clothes were wet, like he'd been walking in the rain, and he was gasping for breath. I looked up at him, my body tense. Jake's eyes would tell me if everything was okay, but he didn't look at me. His eyes were everywhere but on me.

My tail between my legs and my ear flat against my head, I walked back slowly into the room to Jake, who had turned away to kneel on the floor as he cleaned up the mess he'd made. I walked carefully to avoid the mess and nuzzled against his leg, trembling, needing Jake to touch me. What had happened to the boy I loved?

Jake sighed, and his shoulders dropped. Perhaps the anger he brought to each game had proven too much for him. He turned and hugged me, like when I was a pup, his old familiar voice rising above the silence.

"I'm sorry, buddy. I'm so sorry. I'm just scared. I don't know if I can do this. What if I can't make it back?"

Jake began to sob. The words had set him free. He reached out, holding me tight to his unsteady body as if afraid if he let go, he might fall away and never find his way back. We stayed like that a long time, our bodies locked as one, the way we were always meant to be. I nuzzled Jake's face, and his body shuddered, surrendering to the pain that had darkened his life.

"You didn't deserve that. None of you do."

Jake's eyes continued to look everywhere but into mine. He didn't understand the only thing he would see there was love. Something still haunted him.

I could smell fear, but there was more. Jake missed him too, but I never heard his name mentioned. Each day Dad's scent faded more throughout the house, but even while it dimmed, powerful memories of him burned brightly for me. I sighed, lowering my head to Jake's lap. If Dad were here, he'd know what to do. He'd be able to help Jake on his painful journey back to us. But Dad was gone, and Jake had to find his way without the strong, wise man we all loved.

Slowly, Slowly

The changes from day to day were so slight, I might've been the only one to see Jake's improvement. But in time, others could see it too. He began to walk and move better. All the games he played started to make a difference. Finally, My Boy was getting stronger, but the darkness lingered.

One morning, Skyler came by in her car, the top open to the sun. I wagged my tail excitedly. Not to see Skyler because, as usual, she didn't show interest in seeing me, but with Jake moving better, I hoped we might go for a ride. It had been a long time, and this would be a good day to take a nice long drive with the wind blowing in my face and whipping my ear, like running faster than I ever had before. I lay on the step by Jake's side, my tail wagging in anticipation.

But we didn't go anywhere. Instead, Skyler sat down on the steps next to Jake, who stared at the ground, squeezing a ball in his bad hand while Skyler, without greeting me, started to talk. Usually, Skyler babbled on like some of the small dogs I'd encounter on my walks with Jake, yipping and yapping with little to say but with a message that cried out: "Look at me! Look at me! Don't you see me? Aren't I pretty? Aren't I special? I'm here! Notice me!!"

Today, Skyler acted differently. She sat next to Jake, her body tense, her eyes moving about but never looking at Jake. Skyler found one of my old balls in the tall grass and picked it up. Shifting it from one hand to the next, I thought she might want to play but realized, as usual, Skyler wasn't interested in me. I sat quietly, anxious, her mood affecting me as well. At last, she started to speak, her voice halting and uncertain.

"I just got back from freshman orientation and will move in next week. I probably won't be back till Thanksgiving. This isn't how I planned my first year. I figured we'd have so much more freedom and time together. Now, none of that will be happening. You won't be going to Dartmouth or the Air Force Academy. I'm sorry. I mean, well . . . at least not this year, anyway."

Skyler took a deep breath, the words now coming faster.

"I've talked to all my friends and my mother. They all agree. They think it wouldn't be fair to you. Wouldn't be fair to mislead you. To expect you to wait for me."

Skyler dropped the ball and reached out to take Jake's hand.

"I'm sorry, Jake, and I really don't want you to think this is about the accident. I'd hate for you, for *anyone*, to think I was that shallow or unfeeling. The truth is, I ran into Kyle Vandenberg on my first visit to Dartmouth back in the spring. He's a junior majoring in prelaw and good friends with several of the girls at the sorority I'm pledging, and, well, we started talking. We've seen each other a few times over the summer. Nothing has happened. Nothing, I swear, but my mother thinks it would be wrong for you not to know."

Jake's body stiffened, and he turned to look at Skyler. "Let's not drag this out. We've barely seen each other since I got out of the hospital, and each visit's been shorter than the last. I've got no chains on you and won't hold you back out of some misplaced sense of loyalty."

"Damn it, Jake, there you go acting all wounded and noble. I hate when you do that. This has been coming for a long time, long before your accident. I'm going to pledge my mother's sorority, and I know how frivolous you think all that is. Even before the accident, I imagined the excuses I'd have to make about why my boyfriend couldn't go to this dance or that event. You were still talking about the Air Force Academy, and even if you came to Dartmouth, you wouldn't be interested in the things I am. Was I supposed to miss every party and social event you found silly, or just go alone? I'd end up explaining each absence. *Oh, my boyfriend's volunteering at the local soup kitchen or knocking on doors trying to collect money for wounded veterans.* Jeez, Jake, that's why we pay taxes.

"I know this all sounds petty, and things like this shouldn't matter. But I'm not like you. I thought being with you could make me care less about material things and what other people think, but it hasn't. At least not enough. My mom thinks I should be with someone who understands and appreciates the world I come from. I'm sorry, Jake, but I think she's right."

Skyler was crying, and Jake looked like he might start. Neither acted mad. They both just looked very sad. Then Jake spoke.

"I remember the first day I saw you. I thought you were the prettiest girl I'd ever seen, and I told myself, if you were my girl, I'd never want anything else. Then, somehow, I made it happen, or maybe you made it happen. I don't really know anymore. I was in heaven: Skyler Winship, the prettiest, most popular, richest girl in school. Being with you was all I wanted. I forgot about old friends and stopped spending time with my family to be with you. But the more I was with you, the less of *me* there seemed to be.

"Skyler, I want so much out of life and wanted you to be a part of it all. I want to make a difference, touch people, challenge them to dream about making the world better, and running one of your father's car dealerships won't give me that. I thought you shared those dreams. Remember talking about having something more than your mother's cloying dilettante life, with a seat on the board at the museum and playing tennis at the country club? You said you wanted something different for yourself. What's changed?"

Skyler sighed, her voice now tired. "Reality, Jake. Reality changed it. It's easy to fantasize about what could be, to listen as you painted a picture of a life we'd build. It seemed so exciting and different. But it was just talk. I never stopped to think of all the things I'd have to give up. The truth is, I'm not strong enough. I wish I were, but I'm not. I like nice things. I like not having to work for them, and I'm afraid I couldn't handle not having those things or trying to make it on my own.

"Jake, you've never had what I have. You don't understand what I'd be giving up. I can just see you, delighted living in a crowded, tiny third-floor apartment in the Flats, happy to do without vacations or nice things. If I stayed, I'd blame you for everything I didn't have and hate you for not wanting them too. But each day, you'd wake up with that Jake DiSpirito *I'm going to take on the world* smile and never complain.

"I'd end up hating myself, and seeing you would be a painful reminder I wasn't the person you thought I was. And my worst fear, one day, you'd see it too. I want to spare myself the shame of seeing that look in your eyes. Yes, I wanted more than my mother's life. I'm just not willing to take the risks that come with it.

"I did . . . I loved you so. I remember you riding that silly red bike of yours on Country Club Road, knocking on doors, asking if people needed their lawns mowed. You were just so comfortable in your own skin, different from everyone I knew, so calm and kind. Funny, but never at someone else's expense. Boy, was that rare in the circles where I ran, where making others seem small was rule number one. But not you. You didn't care what anyone thought, never blinking as the kids at the white-bread table snickered at you and the greasy, brown-bag lunches your mother made. All while they're sneaking off to McDonald's for burgers and fries. I watched with envy, thinking if I could reach out and grab on to someone with that kind of moral compass, if I could hold on tight enough, maybe I could get away from the people on the Hill. Maybe I could be something better. But I'm not strong enough to break those ties. I loved you, Jake. I did. I just don't think I loved you enough."

Jake got up from the steps and knelt in front of Skyler. He took her hands in his and looked up.

"There's a lot more to you than you think. I saw it when others couldn't. Maybe even when *you* couldn't. I hope you find a way to break from your parents' insulated world. There is so much more out there. But you're right. You didn't love me enough. I guess neither of us loved each other enough.

"I remember telling you I dreamt I walked on water and how real it all felt. Irrational as it seemed, I almost believed I could do it. I sat on the edge of my bed that night, thinking maybe, through some metaphysical kismet, I could do the unimaginable.

"You laughed later when I told you, saying how silly I could be. It's true, but I want . . . no, I *need* someone who loves me so much the inconceivable seems possible and believes in me more than I do. With the world telling us what we can't do, I want the woman I love to believe, together, we can do the impossible."

Crying more than ever, Skyler kissed Jake and stepped away, stopping to hug me fiercely like she never had before.

"I hope you find someone who loves you that much. You deserve it. And Jake, don't settle."

She ran to her car, leaving Jake and me alone on the steps. As she drove away, Jake began to cry, and he kept repeating something over and over: "We are what we think. We are what we think."

Harder and Harder

After that day, Jake worked even harder in the wrestling games. Covered in sweat, Jake drove himself more and more. Never calling him Dave anymore, Jake shouted at Doctor Death, demanding the big man push him further and further while Jake refused to stop in the crazy games they played. When Dougie or Sam visited, Jake challenged them to rough play. Nothing else was on his mind but to drive his body forward. Sam, ever-serious, would calmly talk to Jake as they played so roughly I feared Jake would hurt himself, while Dougie giggled and talked nonstop, shouting to anyone who'd listen.

"Who's the real Doctor Death? Dougie Death, physical trainer extraordinaire! Is that all you've got? DiSpirito, give me more! Young Jake, give me more!"

Whoever was there during the games fueled the burning need in Jake. Seeing him pushed to exhaustion, they'd be stunned, after the briefest of gasping breaks, to hear Jake's croaking voice cry out again, demanding more.

If Jake wasn't playing these physical games, he played new strange word games with Mom or Maria. They didn't seem to be much fun, like the games the family used to play, laughing and shouting as they sat on the floor, moving different markers around a colorful board. I never understood those games, but at least everyone had fun playing, and I got to lie by their side, my head in one of their laps, and enjoy my family.

These new games were different, with a lot less laughter. At first, Jake got mad all the time, which he'd never done playing family games. Before, when the family played, win or lose, Jake laughed and had fun. But with these new, strange games, Jake yelled all the time, getting angry, winning now the only thing that mattered to him. Sometimes Jake yelled at the others, but mostly Jake got mad at himself for not being better. But despite how angry he got, Jake kept playing and playing. Mom or Maria would hold up cards while Jake barked out answers. No matter how angry he got, they'd be by his side, giving encouragement, cheering like they were on the same team.

After Skyler's visit, Jake played all his games more passionately than ever. If Mom or Maria weren't around, he'd get these cards out and shout at them by himself. Sometimes, Jake smiled and nodded his head, calling out his answers. But other times, he'd cry in anger, throwing the cards across the room, only to jump up, limping, and move forward to retrieve the cards to start all over again.

This is how Jake spent his days, each one into the next, playing these wrestling or word games. If someone visited, he'd play with them, and when no one came around, he'd go it alone. If awake, Jake played one of these games, shouting to himself, sometimes in pleasure, often in anger. He only stopped to eat or take me for a walk.

Even our walks became like a demanding contest Jake had to win. He'd pull my leash, pushing me to walk faster and faster. At first, I tried to go slowly. Jake was hurt, and I wanted to protect him, but he wouldn't rest. He kept pushing himself, calling out for me to go, go, demanding more of himself each day. Jake didn't talk on these walks, like we used to. No. Squaring his shoulders, Jake dragged that bad leg while giving my leash that quick snap, constantly challenging me to go, go, go.

Ever so slowly, Jake started to get less angry. Playing the games over and over, he learned and began to play better. Shouts of celebration would rattle our small house when Jake beat Dave in one of their wrestling matches. A smile would light up Jake's face after winning one of those confusing word games, while Mom's tired eyes showed some of her old joy for life. Finally, on our walks, Jake began to drag his leg less and less, so much so I stopped worrying about going too fast. Instead, we ran together, like in the old days. Several times, laughing, he pulled on my leash to slow our pace without getting angry at himself for not being fast enough.

Then, one day, the final sign I was getting My Boy back, Jake, at last, began to talk on our walk.

"I miss him, Bull. I miss him so much. I haven't been able to talk about him. And I'm not proud of how I acted around him the last few years. He was such a powerful presence. I just needed to get away. Dad kept reaching out, and the more he tried, the more I pushed back. So now he's gone, and I can't talk to him . . . now that I want to . . . need to. What's worse, I haven't been there for Mom since the accident. I've shut her out when she's tried to talk. I just couldn't handle it."

We'd stopped on the hillside of the park, my sides heaving from the pace of our walk. Jake picked up a stick, slapping it against his open hand, appearing to study it as he continued.

"She's needed to talk. I just haven't been ready. My feelings about Dad are so complicated. When I was a kid, I thought he was perfect, but as I got older, I could see his flaws and imperfections. He had a hard life, and it affected him. His intensity scared me. He was so hard on himself, on everybody, really, just expecting so much. I felt betrayed for the imperfections I saw and hated myself for judging him. I needed to distance myself. So while he kept pushing to go camping one last time before college, I kept putting it off. I was afraid of what I might say if we were alone like that again.

"I was starting to get my head around it all. Dad was like all of us, human and flawed. He'd battled demons, and it scarred him, and those scars affected how he interacted with the people he loved. Understanding all that was like coming out of a dark tunnel in our relationship, one Dad didn't even know existed. Maybe he sensed it, but I couldn't tell him. Now I never can."

Jake rose from the tall grass where he had been

sitting and stared at the stick in his hand. He sighed, reached back, and with a grunt, threw the stick far off into the distance. But I didn't chase it. My Boy needed me by his side.

Dad was gone. Still, the memories of him were everywhere, none shining more brightly than when I looked at Jake. The way he stood, the special glow in his eyes when he laughed, even the hard tone in his voice when he got angry all made me miss Dad just a little bit less and love Jake that much more.

"It's crazy. One minute he's there. This indomitable presence. And the next minute he's gone. Killed by a drunk driver. He's gone, Bull, but I feel him with me every day. Hell, he's in my head everywhere I go. I'm not proud of how I've acted during my rehab. I've felt pretty sorry for myself and lost my temper a lot. I didn't treat those closest to me very nicely, but all the while, his voice was in the back of my head, challenging me to accept my imperfections and do all I could with the gifts God gave me. Throughout my recovery, I kept hearing his favorite: Did you do your best?

"*Did you do your best?* It's one of my earliest memories. How can you answer that as a kid? I'd stay up nights thinking: Was *that* my best? It didn't matter. School, lacrosse . . . I always figured I must have had just a little more to give. More I could have done. Like I somehow left something in reserve. But not this time. I put everything I have into this recovery, and now it's time for me to do something with this second chance. I'm not going to waste it. But first, I have to make things right with Mom.

"I haven't been there for her, and I don't know how to make it up to her. But a wise man once told me, 'Sometimes you have to take that long walk across the gym floor to ask the girl to dance.' So tonight, I'm going to talk to Mom."

I stirred as his old familiar tone calmed me. The anger gone, a kinder, gentler Jake sat by my side. It had been a long, painful road, but somehow, he had found his way. Just when I thought there was no way I could ever love him more, I watched My Boy become a man.

Making Peace

"Great meal." Jake scraped tasty pieces of meat into my bowl while he spoke to Mom. "Now sit while I do the dishes and tell you about the conversation I had with Bull today."

"Rest while my son, the sphinx, finally speaks? Who could refuse?"

Jake turned to face Mom and shrugged. "Yeah, sorry, that's what I want to talk about. I kind of shut down since the accident, working on my recovery, the breakup with Skyler, and . . ."

"The loss of your father?"

"Yeah, especially that. I wasn't ready to deal with any of it. I was so angry and scared. I spent a lot of time feeling sorry for myself. Then, as the recovery started coming along, I focused on that and blocked everything else out. I was afraid to think about Dad and what it all meant to me.

"It's hard to admit, but the last few years, all I wanted to do was get out from under his shadow. Sometimes I almost hated him and then hated myself for feeling that way. I'd lie in bed at night wishing he was gone, afraid of measuring up to his expectations."

Jake's voice sounded strong and confident when he began talking, but now he struggled. He dropped his head and leaned against the wall, lowering himself to the ground till he sat on the floor. Then, with his shoulders sagging, he buried his face in his hands and began to cry. He tried to speak, but no words came, and he surrendered to his pain. His crying grew into long, tortuous sobs, and Mom rushed to him, her eyes sharing in his pain. She dropped to the floor by his side and pulled Jake into her arms, cradling him in her lap. Mom rocked back and forth, holding him tightly to quell his pain as Jake's sadness overwhelmed him.

"Ssssh, sssh. It's okay, honey. It's okay. It's going to be okay."

I hurried over to be by his side, but Jake didn't notice, his pain blinding him to everything around him. After the longest time, Jake pulled himself up straight, gave Mom a long hug, and began to speak again.

"I'm sorry. I'm so ashamed of what I felt, all the things I didn't say to Dad, and it's worse knowing I haven't been there for you. Now it's too late to change any of it."

Mom took his face in her hands and looked straight at him.

"Honey, your father knew you loved him, and he loved you more than life. Yes, he wanted to spend time with you as you got older, but he realized the shadow he cast. Your father was no saint, but he was a good man. He loved you no matter what you did. He just didn't know how to celebrate the small victories of life. He constantly challenged himself and the people he loved to strive for more. I know how exhausting that could be, but it came from a place of love. Never more so than with you.

"Your father didn't live in the past or worry about what might have been. He always looked to the next challenge, the next opportunity. He's gone, but he wouldn't want us wallowing over the mistakes we made. He'd expect us to look to the future. So, my son, what will you do with this second chance you have?"

Mom's words brought a small smile to Jake's face.

"Wow, I thought Dad was the taskmaster. But you're right. It's time for me to get back to work."

Jake stood up, running his hand across my back, and led Mom to the table. "I've been thinking about some of the things Anthony said after getting clean. He spoke about how making amends to the people he hurt was a critical part of the twelve-step recovery program. I realize I owe lots of people apologies. And that starts with you. Dad would want me to look forward, but first, I have to say a few things to the people who stood by me when I was hard to be around. I've had days I'm not proud of. I felt sorry for myself, lost my temper at the smallest of things. I didn't treat those closest to me very nicely, but even in my darkest moments, I felt his presence guiding me. A voice in my head challenging me to give it all I had, accept my imperfections, and do all I could with the gifts God gave me. It was Dad's voice and . . . yours."

Jake took Mom's hands and continued. "I know I

haven't shown it, but I did listen . . . to both of you. I'm sorry I wasn't there for you. I can't imagine how alone you must have felt. And you're right. I can't undo that. But I promise I'm here now, and I'm not going anywhere. Whatever you need, I'll be there. It took a long time to get my head straight, and there are more hard days to come, but I'm going to live a life that will make both you and Dad proud."

Now it was Mom's turn to cry. "Losing your father was a pain unlike anything I'd ever known, and then, for close to a year, I was afraid I lost you too. I won't lie. You haven't been easy to be around. At times you were downright miserable."

Mom smiled and wiped away a tear. "Through it all, I saw so much of your father's strength in you. I'm so proud of how hard you worked, but we need to put that pain behind us. I don't know what you'll do, but it's time to pay back for all you've been given. It's time to go out and make a difference in people's lives. Leave the world a better place. Your father did that, and he'd expect nothing less from you."

Mom had spoken in a tone I knew well. And Jake listened. He rose from the table and gave her a long hug. He had that look in his eye. Time to go to work. But I'm not sure even Jake knew what that work would be.

A Door Opens

Footsteps fell on the front walk. My ear perked, and I barked, alerting my family of a visitor. Our doorbell rang, mixing with the sound of my warning. The man in the long white shirt who'd helped Jake back at the big, scary house when he was hurt so badly, stood in our doorway. He wore a regular-size shirt, and he didn't have that distinctive smell all the helpers at the giant house had. But I still recognized him immediately with his familiar, alert eyes and unique voice that sounded different from the people I knew. The moment Jake opened the door, the man dropped low to the ground and called out to me. I spun around in a friendly hello, barked, then jumped forward to greet him.

"Hello, Bull. Today we get to play. Unfortunately, the only thing hospitals frown on more than dogs wandering their halls is their surgeons petting them. But no rules now, and I get to play with you all I want."

I settled close to him, and he scratched my chest with two firm, perceptive hands. I decided I'd made a new friend. He expertly rubbed my chest and looked up to smile at Mom, who now stood at the front door next to Jake.

Mom gave the man a big hug, welcoming him to our home. She hurried him into the house, gave him a drink, and placed all kinds of food in front of him before he even had a chance to sit. Then he settled in a chair with me sitting by his side, and the man scratched gently behind the nub of my ear as if studying it.

"So, Bull, I hear our patient has made tremendous progress, proving how fallible doctors are and what belief in something bigger than ourselves can accomplish."

The man looked at Mom, a smile growing, and he nodded his head as if he approved of something Mom said, but her lips had never moved. Then he turned to Jake.

"You're looking great. I spoke to Doctor Orlofsky. I hear your fine motor skills are back to ninety-five percent, and the worst of the memory issues are behind you. He says there's a bit of vision degradation in your left eye, but in total, an amazing recovery. Congratulations. Learning the alphabet, multiplication tables, and more was hard enough the first time. Reacquiring those skills as an adult after the kind of trauma your brain endured is nothing short of miraculous. I hope you don't mind, but I also checked in with Dave Slaughter and your other physical trainers. They say your PT effort has been Herculean. But after my talk with your mother the day you came out of your coma, I expected nothing less. You may start college a year later than planned, but I expect you'll accomplish great things, just like she predicted."

He stayed and ate with our family that night, with Mom continually putting more food on his plate as he patted his small round stomach, pleading for her to stop. It was a fun night, with lots of laughter around the table, especially after Sam and Dougie stopped by. The man, Doctor Yoshida or Tama, as Mom called him, remembered them, especially Dougie, and everyone laughed whenever Dougie spoke. After the boys came, Mom switched her attention to feeding them, and Dougie stopped talking only when food filled his mouth. But through the night, Mom kept repeating things like: "I can't thank you enough, Doctor. I told you, this boy's made of something special."

Yes, everyone enjoyed that night, but no one more than me, as I got to eat several meals because Doctor Yoshida kept slipping food off his plate for me. Then his voice grew serious.

"Mrs. DiSpirito, you told me Jake would leave a mark in life, and getting to know him, I agree. Buddhists believe the soul is eternal, and our goal is to grow and learn. We hope our soul comes back wiser from each incarnation. It can take many lifetimes, but we believe the spirit evolves to one of perfect purity with the energy in the universe. It's heady stuff, but I believe it deeply, and that belief guides my life.

"I also believe, on rare occasions, you can glimpse a past incarnation. Sometimes people sense a much older soul in a young person. I see a very old soul in Jake. He'll make a mark with this second chance. And I think I've come upon one small way he might help others. After all, isn't that why we're all here?"

The doctor turned to face Jake. "If you'd be willing, I'd like you to come to the hospital and talk with some of the kids in the trauma center."

Jake coughed, trying to swallow the last bit of food he had in his mouth, and then smiled. My tail whipped across the floor. I'd not seen My Boy smile that wide in a long time.

"Wow, Doc. You just gave me chills. Your timing is scary. My vision and motor skills issues aren't deal-breakers for the Air Force Academy, but I'd lose another year. The delay's gnawing at me. My life's been knocked off its tracks, and now that I'm back, I don't want to lose any more time. I need to get going." Jake paused to look at Mom. "I was talking with my mother about what I wanted to do with my life and finding a way to give back. The more we talked, the less sure I was going to the academy and learning to fly was still right for me. There may be a different path for me, and working with kids might be a part of it."

Jake grew quiet and stared at his hands, as if they held a secret, then turned to look into the doctor's eyes.

"But I have a big question. I'm touched you think I could help others, but I don't know if I have anything worth saying. During my rehab, I saw many kids in much worse shape than me, with little chance of a positive prognosis for a conventional happy ending. So what could I possibly offer these kids?"

"Damn the prognosis, Jake. Your recovery is

proof we, so-called medical experts, aren't infallible. And sometimes, giving in to a higher power, believing in something bigger than yourself while harnessing a will that refuses to quit, can make miracles happen. You have a message worth sharing. Regardless of their prognosis, you can help many of these kids.

"Now, if I've learned anything from the bone-numbingly boring medical lectures I've attended, the key to being a great speaker is to get people's attention. And you've got one hundred and twenty pounds of attention-grabbing love resting at our feet. I've seen the effect Bull's presence had on you and others at the hospital. I believe your message, with Bull for an opening act, could be a wonderful recipe to motivate and put a smile back on these kids' faces."

I heard my name and leaped up. With my tail held high, I barked and spun in a circle several times, then raced over for a quick pet from Jake before going back to place my head in our guest's lap, where I received more good ear scratches. My new friend laughed.

"That's right, Bull. I'm talking about you. Jake, I hoped you'd say yes, so I took the liberty of registering Bull into a program at the hospital for licensing as a therapy dog. They'll test Bull to confirm he is suited for the work, but I'm confident he's up for the challenge. Bull's exceptionally well-socialized, quick to follow your instructions, and he seems to respond well when hit with unfamiliar stimuli. He doesn't get flustered by lots of noise or crowded rooms. I think he's got the makings of a terrific therapy dog. I love all dogs, but there's something exceptional about this big guy. Like with you, I sense Bull is a very old soul who's learned much in his past journeys. It would be wrong not to share his wonderful spirit with others. I'm convinced just seeing Bull and listening to your story could do wonders for many of these patients."

I sat by my new friend's side while he continued to pet me. He stopped for a moment and again ran his hand across the nub of my ear. Then he took my face in his two hands and looked into my eyes, his thumb trailing along the lines of the scars on my face from my battle with the giant. His eyes grew distant, like he was thinking of a forgotten pain. But then he smiled. Perhaps he, too, understood the power of love to deal with sorrow.

As so often was the case, Jake drew people into our lives. *Good* people. And I knew, somehow, Jake's spirit had brought this kind, thoughtful man back into our lives. Then, with a final touch of my damaged ear, his eyes grew bright once more, and he spoke again.

"Yes. Jake, I think you and Bull can help some people."

PART V

Back to School

Time passed, and Jake went back to that school place, but it was different. They called it college, and he wasn't gone all day. Now, he often went to school at night, or sometimes early in the morning, and he didn't dress up for work, like when Skyler was still coming around.

Jake had a truck now, and I got to go with him, like long ago when I used to race alongside his bike up to the big houses. I didn't ride in the back of Jake's truck like other dogs. No, Jake filled the back with machines or tree branches. So I rode up front next to Jake while we drove up the Hill back to where Skyler lived in her big house surrounded by other big houses. In the old days, Jake knocked on the doors of many places, talking to the people, but now he just started working around people's yards, cleaning them up. He had lots of houses we came back to again and again without even talking to the people unless they came out while we were working to say hello to Jake and pet me. Sometimes Sam or Dougie helped him, but Sam was often away at this college place, and we saw him a lot less. Eventually, Maria went to college too, and we saw her even less.

But for me, the visits Jake and I made to the big house where Jake stayed when he got hurt were the most important thing we did. I learned that huge place was called a hospital, and lots of different people went there when they were hurt or sick and needed to get better.

Before we started going on our visits, Jake and I spent a lot of time playing a whole bunch of new games. At first, they seemed silly, but I discovered they were helping me be ready to visit the hurt and sick children. The games weren't much different than the ones we played when I was a pup, and Jake had taught me how to be his Best Boy. But learning came easier for me now that I was older and less excitable. I learned to stay extra calm, even if someone like Dougie snuck into the room and made a loud noise or if he accidentally poked me when I didn't expect it. Sometimes, the game required me just to sit and wait for a long time while Dougie raced around the room, throwing toys, dropping food, or, well, just acting like Dougie. Then Jake would reward me with a long hug and call me his Best Boy.

One day, Jake covered my back with a bright cloth. I shook, trying to knock it off. Having something hanging over me didn't feel natural. Why would Jake do it? Was he trying to show dominance, like when a mother puts her mouth on her pup's neck to make the puppy behave, or when a more powerful dog stands over another dog to show he's in charge? Jake and I didn't treat each other like that. It didn't make sense. Now more than ever, with the new games we'd played, Jake knew I would always behave. So why did he put this strange thing on me?

After that day, Jake put the cloth on me each time we practiced, and I grew more comfortable with it. And then, the first time we went to the hospital, it all made sense. The cloth was like the uniform Dad used to wear to work each day. It allowed me into the hospital to see the kids where I could work, helping these children and the other sick people feel better. Jake put that coat on me because he loved me and knew I'd be good at helping the people who needed it. Once again, life showed me how lucky I was that Jake was mine.

Now, nothing pleased me more than going to the hospital and hearing Jake call me his Best Boy while I let the children hug and sometimes accidentally poke or prod me. No poke, loud noise, or harsh smell could undo the pleasure of being there. And for the first time, I had something equally important as praise from Jake. It was the sound of the children's squealing voices when they saw us come into the room. Jake and I were helping them. I loved my job, and I loved Jake even more for helping me to do it. Spending time with these sick and hurting children wasn't a job they'd let just any dog do, and Jake's faith in me had helped make this important work happen.

After our visits, I enjoyed the long ride home with Jake by my side, feeling the wind as I held my nose out the window, content and happy. We had helped those children smile and made their lives just a little better.

Jake and I were both Best Boys.

Jake continued to go to school when he wasn't working with his truck up on the Hill. Sometimes, he'd take Carlos and José, Maria's brothers, who were both almost taller than him, to help with the work around the big houses. Still, Jake made time to visit the hospital and other places where sick, injured, or sad people needed to see us. We met many people, but I enjoyed it most when we visited the children.

Some children were very sick, growing weaker by the day, while others improved with each visit. Regardless of how sick they were, their bright eyes and smiles showed we were helping them, even if only for a moment. Sometimes the children wrestled roughly with me, while other times, I'd sit by a young child's side, their hand on my head, unmoving, as I listened to their unsteady breathing. Some were so sick I feared I might never see them again, and I lingered longer, trying to ease their pain. Visiting the sickest children made me feel empty and strange, but I wanted to be there for them while they lay in pain, struggling to breathe. Jake was always by my side, sharing in my sadness, his strength helping me do my job.

Soon enough, it would be time to move on to visit other children, who squealed with joy at the sight of me and rushed to greet us, ready to play. With my tail flopping madly, I'd suffer accidental pokes or prods. Whatever the children needed, we were happy to be there, to see those eyes grow wide with wonder the moment we entered a room.

Old friends drifted away. We rarely saw Maria or Sam, while other friends became more frequent parts of our lives. At the hospital, we saw Doctor Yoshida a lot, and sometimes Anthony came to visit a sick friend who needed to talk.

Anthony was much better now. Those sad memories that used to frighten him so terribly were no longer controlling his life. Often, Anthony came by the house when Jake was at school to take me for long walks. He also took me to the building where Dad used to drop him off when Anthony had trouble walking. It was the place Anthony went when we found him wandering the streets so angry and confused he'd shout at strangers, afraid and imagining they wanted to hurt him.

Going into that building, Anthony would put my bright blanket on me, signaling I was there to help people, like at the hospital. These people were a different kind of sick, but I could still smell their fear. They sat in groups and listened to each other, taking turns talking. Some got angry and shouted or banged their chairs, while others cried. Others stared off with unfocused, frightened eyes. Unwilling to speak, these people had pain deep inside them that no one could touch, and they'd sit in silence, suffering. Like at the hospital, my job was to be there for them, let them pet me, or maybe just lie by their side to help them stay calm.

Anthony always stayed in the room with me. He'd try to get people to talk and help calm the angry ones. The way he said things and the confident tone of his voice sounded like Dad. Anthony was saying the same kind of things Dad talked to him about long ago when he felt so sick. These familiar words brought me closer to Anthony and made me feel like Dad still stood close by.

One day, I'd spent the afternoon with Anthony visiting his sad friends, then returned home to have dinner with Mom.

"Bull was great today." Anthony reached down to pet me as he talked. "One of our vets, Walter, has struggled with lots of anger and mood swings since he returned from Iraq. Walter started talking and began to open up about some painful stuff. It was a big step for him. But he tensed up, struggling again. He shut down, going back into his shell, closed off from any chance of help. Then, out of the corner of my eye, I see Bull get up from where he'd been lying, walk over, and rest his head in Walter's lap. I don't know if it registered with Walter, but he put his hand on Bull's head and let it slide down to start scratching Bull's ear. You know, the one that's kinda all chewed up? Walter paused for a moment, like he was thinking, then laughed, mumbled something about us all having scars, and picked up talking where he'd left off. Walter shared for another ten minutes and opened up about some things that had been haunting him for a very long time."

Anthony took my face in his hands and stared into my eyes. "How did you grow to be so wise?" Then he looked back at Mom. "You know the program. For the rest of our lives, it's gonna be *one day at a time.* But Walter made a breakthrough today, and I don't know if it could have happened if Bull hadn't been there for him. It was a beautiful thing to see. I swear, Bull knew what he was doing."

Mom got up from the table and gave Anthony a big hug.

"It's remarkable how many people Bull's touched. Of course, I could never prove it, but I think Bull knows exactly what he's doing. We're very proud of Bull, but I hope you know how proud I am of you. John would be too. My husband never held back. If he were here now, he'd tell you how much he respected you for the courage you've shown in taking your life back."

Mom kept mentioning Dad, and I could tell she was talking about important things. Jake came home, and he joined us while Mom continued talking about our family and the love we all shared.

Mom finished and gave Anthony another big hug. His eyes were wet, but Mom's words had pleased him.

"I am proud of the work I do and hope I'm affecting others' lives. But I have no illusions. Many people helped me along the way. John challenged me to go back to school to get my MSW but, most importantly, to stick with the twelve-step program. I wouldn't be where I am and helping others if it weren't for him. So I owe it to John and the others who helped me to try to help those I can. Giving back through my counseling and working as an AA sponsor is the least I can do."

Anthony stopped petting me and stared at the darkness outside our window for a long time before speaking again.

"At my worst, I said some pretty ugly things to John. I was scared and blamed everyone else for the problems in my life. When I hit bottom, I became the worst version of myself. Filled with anger, I called John every vile thing I could imagine. I thought if I could hurt him badly enough, he'd give up and leave me alone to wallow in my despair and self-hate. I screamed at him and asked why he even bothered with me, his sobriety, any of it. I said life wasn't worth living, and we should both just crawl back into a bottle and drink until we die.

"He exploded. A side of him I'd never seen before. He got in my face with his fists clenched. I swear, he was going to take a swing at me. I'm half a head taller and forty pounds heavier than him, but man, he scared me. That look in his eyes. . . .

"Then, like he threw a switch, he composed himself, apologized, and started to talk in that calm, rational way he had. He talked about life being a gift. And how ashamed he was at the way he almost threw his life away, and that's why my talking of the worthlessness of life angered him so. He said we should celebrate each moment, and the greatest thanks anyone could give for the blessing of life was to leave the world a better place. I'm proof John did that with his life, and now I'll do all I can to do the same in memory of that wonderful, flawed man who helped me to accept my own imperfections."

Jake tried to speak but stopped as tears filled his eyes, and Mom wrapped her arms around Anthony, lowering her head and crying. Sadness flowed from all of them, but while each sat deep in their thoughts, I felt a hint of joy slip into the room and linger over us.

Talking about Dad often made everyone smile

and cry at the same time. We all missed Dad terribly, but as the sadness slowly faded, a soft wind rustled the curtains, and a breeze caressed my face. Something told me our story wasn't over.

Maria's News

My ear shot up at familiar footfalls on the walkway approaching our house. My nose twitched, confirming what my ears already knew. Maria stood outside. Before she knocked, I raced past Mom to meet her at the door, spinning round and round, barking a delight-filled greeting to my old friend.

Mom opened the door, and I bolted past her, pouncing on Maria, who fell to the ground at the top of the stairs and let me lavish her with affection. She laughed a wonderfully throaty sound reminiscent of her girlish giggles. Her laughter was no less happy now, yet something had changed. It was more in control and self-assured than the laugher of the little girl I'd grown up loving.

Maria came into the house, kissed Mom on both cheeks, and began to talk. I brushed against Maria, her familiar smell warming me, but it seemed like two people had come to visit. The lovely childhood friend I remembered so well was still there, scratching under my chin and smiling her familiar smile. But behind her bright eyes, someone new and even happier had joined us. Maria spoke a bit more calmly, moved just a bit more slowly, with a self-assured, gentle confidence that reminded me of someone else.

I rested my head in Maria's lap while she and Mom talked, and she leaned forward to give me some of those wonderful chest scratches I loved so much. Calmed by Maria's presence, I nuzzled against her, trying to understand the change. I finally did when she and Mom laughed together. Maria, my childhood friend, the most wonderful girl I'd ever known, had grown up and now had the strength, manner, and gentle carriage of the most extraordinary woman I knew.

This new, older, wiser Maria reminded me of Mom in all her strength and dignity. She held her head high, shoulders square, answering Mom's questions with a calm, self-confident voice.

A truck pulled up. A door slammed closed, and my joy grew boundless. Jake had come home from work. With Jake and Maria about to be together again, my family was complete. I jumped from the floor and met Jake at the door, barking a joyful greeting. The room's calm was lost to my excitement at having my friends back, like when we were young.

Jake dropped to the ground in the doorway to wrestle, surprised at my excitement.

"Whoa, buddy, it's only been a few hours." Jake smiled widely, locking me in his powerful arms, ready to battle. Then I was free, Jake no longer on the floor. He stood up, noticing Maria for the first time.

"Oh, hey, kid, I heard you were back in town. How you doing?"

"I'm good. Commencement last week, and now time for the real world. Need to find a job. I'd love to work in an intensive care unit, which means someplace like Mass General or the Brigham. I'll have a long commute, but the work will inspire me."

With Jake's arrival, the grown-up Maria faded, and some of the little girl reappeared in her voice.

"Meantime, I'm moving in with my papa. Need to save some money, and he can use an extra pair of eyes on the twins. Plus, it'll be good to see Diego more. Thanks for throwing some work the twins' way. I know they liked having the extra money in their pockets, and Dad's happy they're busy."

"Happy to. They're good workers, although Carlos can talk your ear off. I think the exposure to Dougie in his formative years irreparably affected him."

Everyone smiled at the mention of Dougie's name, but Jake's voice lacked its usual calm.

"Bull and I see Diego whenever we can, at the group home, Pham's, or your house, if he's visiting your pop."

Maria nodded. "Diego's always talking about Jake's latest visit and what you guys have done, going to the movies or out to eat. I can't thank you enough. It means the world to Papa too."

"Hey, you guys are family. It's nothing."

Jake stood in the doorway, and I kept wondering why he didn't come to sit with us.

"Jake, Maria has some other news." Mom got

up, walked behind Maria, and placed her hands on Maria's shoulder.

"Yes . . . um. Well, I'm . . . I'm engaged."

"Wow, engaged." Jake's voice sounded strange and lacking in its usual relaxed confidence. He stepped away from the wall and lowered himself into a small chair by the door, looking everywhere but at Maria. "Yeah, great news. I mean, for you. Great news. So, who's the lucky guy? Do we know him? Wow, little Maria Fuentes engaged. That's, that's . . . just great."

They talked a while longer, but the mood in the room had changed. Jake drifted further away, even while sitting across from us, and Maria sat tapping her feet and staring at her hands. It wasn't long before she got up. She gave Mom a long, hard embrace and a quick sideways hug to Jake before calling me over and giving me a powerful hug that frightened me with its intensity.

Maria hurried out the door, leaving me to listen to her familiar footfalls on the walk, carrying her away from our house.

I brushed against Jake's leg, but he didn't reach out to touch me. Maybe he too was listening to the familiar footsteps rushing away from us.

Having a Party

I stirred, the activity around me a sure signal we were going to have visitors. Lots of visitors. Mom had been cooking for days and kept coming into the house with more bags. The countertops overflowed with food, and mouthwatering scents were everywhere. This party might be the biggest ever. Dougie and Sam both stopped by. Sam, back from that college place, was around all the time again, his calm, strong presence pleasing me more than ever. The boys brought lots of extra chairs and set them up around the house and yard. They also covered the backyard in one of those giant cloths, like the one we'd sleep in when we went off into the woods. But this one was much, much bigger and open on the sides.

The twins and Diego came by, bringing lots of additional food and helping the others who were hurrying around the house, following Mom's instructions. Maria's scent was evident on all the cooked food they brought, but there was no sign of her. There rarely was. When I walked by her house with Jake, I could smell her presence, but she never came out to see me. A few times, when Jake was busy, Mom took me out, and magically, Maria appeared, showing all her old delight at being with me.

Jake had been away for several days, and everyone worked around the house while I anxiously paced from the front door to the windows, searching for any sign of My Boy. Mom kept mentioning the words *interview*, *New York*, and *big job*, but it made no sense to me. I wondered why he'd leave our loving family, but I guess humans and dogs can be similar in that way. Sometimes dogs get distracted by a new smell or sight and wander off from their family. Usually, it's just in the park or near the giant water, but when a gate is left open, or if the dog can dig a hole under a fence, they might go exploring on a bit of adventure. Not so long ago, I'd smelled a new dog in the neighborhood, and I wiggled though a hole I dug to introduce myself. I guess I was gone for a while because Mom and Jake acted very excited to see me when I returned. Sometimes my little adventures might last through the night, but I never failed to find my way home, and I had to trust Jake to do the same.

After days of activity, friends and family filled our house and yard. Nonna and Nonno came from that Florida place. Nonna Connie was there too, sitting with Uncle Frank, who reminded me so much of Dad, the ever-watchful, intense eyes, crooked smile, and deep, strong laugh. Maria's whole family was there, and she came with someone named Stephen. They both acted uncomfortable, barely eating while they stood around, shifting from one foot to another. Maria smiled and relaxed a bit when I came over to say hello. But her friend, who smelled like cat, never petted me, and they left very early while our party remained filled with friends and laughter.

Even Skyler stopped by. She stood off to the side talking to Dougie and Sam for a short time before walking over to Jake to give him a long hug. Skyler spoke with Jake briefly before slipping back to where Dougie and Sam stood talking. When she left, Jake was quite busy with all the people who wanted to speak to him, but he saw her turn to go, and he smiled a goodbye. Skyler stopped by my side to give me a brief hug. Then she looked past the crowd as she walked out of the backyard. She held her head high, but her shoulders slipped forward, and I felt a lingering sadness leave with Skyler, like she was thinking of something she had lost long ago.

Someone called my name, and I trotted over to greet a new guest. I was a happy dog. I brushed against the side of many old friends, feeling hands reach down to graze along my flank. Walking around the yard, I was delighted with the attention and affection, not to mention the treats accidentally, and purposefully, offered up for me.

At last, tired from all my visiting, I stopped in the far corner of the yard and lay down beside Jake, who sat listening to Doctor Yoshida.

"So, your mom says you received a terrific offer, but you haven't committed. So, are you going to accept?"

"Don't know. It's a great opportunity, and the

money's terrific. Everyone's telling me I should jump at the chance."

"But something's holding you back."

"Yes. Not sure what it is. New York's less than an hour's flight out of Logan. I could be home regularly. It's a great job, and the work's important, but I'm not sure I want to spend my life doing clinical research."

Jake petted me, but he appeared distracted. He always managed to find just the right spot, but tonight my ears were begging to be scratched, and he never got to them. So I rubbed my head against his leg and moved over to Doctor Yoshida while Jake continued to talk.

"I minored in education, sort of for a backup, but the more I think about how I want to spend my life, I feel like I belong in the front of a classroom or one-on-one working with kids. I'd make less money, but it feels right, and it would give me the time to work on the writing I've always talked about. Who knows if anything I have to say would be of interest to others. It feels like the height of hubris to think anyone would pay to read what I write, but I think I might have a story or two worth telling, and I want to give it a shot."

"Those are some good reasons for you not to take the research job, but is there something you're not talking about?"

Jake laughed one of his *that's not funny* laughs and shifted in his chair. "Okay, Doc, more proof of your varied skills. Not only are you a terrific surgeon, but you'd make a top-notch therapist. There is more." Jake looked around at the crowded yard and gestured with his hand. "This is home, and this is my family, the people in this town. I belong here. I'm not afraid to leave. I just don't want to. It's like when I decided not to go away for college. I feel like I belong here with the people who came to be with us today."

"Anyone in particular? I thought I saw some glances cast toward a certain dark-eyed young lady a little earlier. Might that be holding you back?"

My back leg started thumping. Our friend had found the perfect spot behind my ear that needed attention, setting my leg in motion. Doctor Yoshida's words got Jake going too, and Jake's legs started bouncing like he had an itch even bigger than mine.

"Just like I said, Doc. A top-notch therapist. But that ship's sailed. People warned me. My parents and friends tried to tell me, but I was too young to see what I had right in front of me. So I acted like an idiot and turned the only woman who could hold a candle to my mother into a friend. So now Maria's marrying someone else, not even knowing how I feel. Pretty dumb, huh. Some valedictorian I turned out to be."

"Jake, I've failed twice at marriage. I could blame my career, but ultimately I placed priorities in the wrong place. I'm no one to give advice, but I remember when you were in the hospital so broken, I worried about the quality of life you'd have. Your mother told me there was no quit in you, and you'd leave your mark in this life. She was right. I didn't know you then, but I do now. And letting someone he cares deeply for walk out of his life without even saying how he feels is not what I'd expect from the son of Anna DiSpirito."

"Ouch, Doc. So much for your famous bedside manner."

"Doctors need a bedside manner. A *friend's* job is to speak the truth. Today, I'm speaking as your friend."

Jake looked up and smiled, seeing Anthony walk toward us with Camille, a woman he had brought to the house before. Jake stood to greet them, his conversation with Doctor Yoshida over. But for the rest of the night, Jake acted strangely, like years ago when he used to look up and stare at that silver bird racing across the sun-streaked sky. My Boy continued to smile and talk to our friends and family, but I could tell he was thinking about something else. I'd heard Maria's name mentioned in Jake's conversation with Doctor Yoshida, and Jake's voice sounded odd when he spoke of her. Jake continued to smile with each new conversation, but his eyes darted around the backyard as if looking for someone who got away. Long into the evening, after all the conversations, hugs, and kisses, the image of Maria coming with her friend Stephen to quickly say hello and just as quickly leave was a memory that wouldn't fade.

Something had happened, or maybe hadn't happened, between Jake and Maria. Something caused the two people I loved so much never to see each other anymore, and when they did, they had nothing to say. So my old friends, who I'd watched grow up together, side by side, friends who never tired of talking, laughing, teasing, yes, and sometimes arguing, now acted like strangers to each other.

The humans I loved could be so peculiar. No dog ever leaves an old friend ungreeted. A friend is a friend forever, and we never miss an opportunity to greet, sniff, or have a play. But, as I've said, dogs are smarter than humans in many ways. I loved Jake, despite the things he couldn't see. Maybe my love could help him find the answers slipping away from him.

Stop and Listen

Our lives went back to normal. Jake left early for work most days but didn't take me with him like he used to. He didn't have the truck anymore. But that was okay because I couldn't jump in and out of it easily, like long ago, and I was content to find a sunny spot in the house to take a long nap while I waited for Jake and Mom to come home.

We moved slower on our walks now, and I'd linger by Maria's house, trying to catch a scent of her. But I could find no sign of a recent visit, so I'd drift past, glancing back until shadows of other houses hid her small home from view. Jake always walked slower when we passed her place, never rushing me to move on. Was he looking for Maria? Perhaps he, too, hoped she might see us and race out to play.

One morning on our walk, we saw Diego. Like Maria, Diego didn't live there anymore. His scent had faded, leaving only faint reminders of my friend. But today, approaching the house, my nose twitched. I stopped in front of their small yard and barked, looking toward their front door until Diego, smiling widely, stepped onto their stairs. My tail thumped from side to side, and Jake released my leash. Diego fell to his knees, clapping his hands, and I raced over to him, licking his face. Then, after lots of hugs, Diego rose and sat next to Jake on the steps of the house. I plopped down at their feet while the old friends talked.

"Good to see you, Diego. Surprised you're visiting on a Saturday. Figured you'd be working at Pham's."

"Maria's gettin' married, and she wants all of us to wear special suits, so Papa's takin' me and the twins to rent some. How dumb's that? Who rents clothes?" Diego had his angry voice, and he paused a moment to point at Jake. "Ya know, I'm mad at you, Jake. Really, really mad."

"Sorry, buddy, but it's not my idea to make you wear a tuxedo."

"That's not why I'm mad. I'm mad at you cuz you're lettin' Stephen marry Maria. What a dumb name that is anyway. Stephen. Ugh. You're suppoz to marry Maria. Always were. And now you're just standin' by and lettin' ugh Stephen marry her."

"Sorry, Diego, but Maria's in love with Stephen and has decided she wants to marry him. You have to respect that. Besides, he seems like a nice guy."

"Nice guy? He doesn't even like *dogs*. How nice a guy can you be if you don't like dogs? Maria loves dogs. You love dogs. He has a cat. A cat! And he yells when he talks at me, like I'm deaf. I told him I was in a special class when I was in school, but it wasn't cuz I can't hear good. See that, you laughed. He didn't even get my joke. He is boooring. And you're lettin' Maria marry him. Marryin' boooring Stephen. How can you do that to her?"

"Diego, she loves him. I'm sorry, there is nothing I can do about that."

"She loves *you*, Jake. She always has. You're just too dumb to see. Sorry. I know we aren't suppoz to call people names or tell them they're dumb, but that's what you are. Dumb, dumb, dumb."

Nobody was better than Jake at calming Diego down and putting a smile back on his face when he got upset, but today was different. Diego did all the talking while Jake sat on their front steps with little to say. Finally, after a long silence, Jake got up, said goodbye, and slowly headed back to our house. Our planned walk forgotten. I couldn't remember Jake walking so slowly and unsure of himself, not since his terrible accident so long ago.

Jake stumbled to his room, forgetting to close the front door or take my leash off. Sitting on the edge of his bed, he stared off at nothing, unaware of my attempts to burrow my snout under his locked fingers or run my flank against his leg.

Finally, after the longest time, Jake rolled onto his side, tension obvious in every part of his body. I jumped onto the bed to lie next to him, relieved when he turned to hug me before closing his eyes and falling into a fitful slumber.

My Boy needed help.

He stirred once in his sleep, and one lone drop fell from his eye. I licked it away. We stayed that way the rest of the afternoon while Jake's breathing slowly slipped into an unsteady rhythm. I slept too, not opening my eyes until the sun completed its journey across the room and sat low in the sky, leaving the house in darkness.

~ ~ ~ ~

"Jake, Jake, are you okay? Jake, the front door's wide open."

Mom woke us from our restless slumber, and Jake stumbled down the hall. Rubbing his eyes, he greeted her.

"Hey, Mom, sorry, yeah, wasn't feeling all that great. Went out early this morning and grabbed a breakfast burrito at a gas station. Guess it didn't agree with me. Feeling much better now."

"Hum. You've got the constitution of a mountain goat. Is that all it is?"

"I'm fine. Guess I'm getting older and can't handle junk food like I used to. Really, it's nothing." Jake fell into the chair across from Mom, his hands folded across his hard, flat stomach.

"Jake, you've been in a funk for weeks. Are you sure nothing else is bothering you? Maybe . . . Maria?"

"Jeez, Ma, not you too. First, Doc Yoshida, and today I get an earful from Diego. Maria and I are friends. Never been anything but good friends. I know it, and she knows it. So why can't other people understand and accept that?"

"Lord, how could I have raised such a blind fool for a son?"

"What do you mean by that?"

Jake's sharp voice startled me, and I looked up,

panting, unsure of what caused Jake's anger.

It seemed he'd tried to avoid something for a long time, but the people who cared for Jake wouldn't let him, and now Mom took her turn. Could this be the help Jake needed? I only hoped this talk didn't leave Jake sadder than the others had. Mom's loving voice reminded me of the sound in Jake's voice when he helped me get ready to visit the children in the hospital.

That voice said *I care and want what's best for you*.

Jake shifted in his chair. He heard it too, but it only made him more anxious.

Mom's eyes narrowed. I knew that look—time for Jake to listen.

"What I mean, my foolishly obtuse son is that beautiful girl has been in love with you since she was six years old. She kept me whole when you were in the hospital, so broken it filled me with desperation and fear. Maria told me everything would be okay. She said you'd been too foolish to see it, but one day she was going to marry you, and you two would give me beautiful grandchildren."

Jake shifted in the chair, raising his head, his alert eyes bright for the first time in a long while. "What? I never knew that."

"She's been right there in front of you for close to twenty years. Maria hung around the house at every opportunity, cooked your favorite foods, joined you and Bull on every walk she could. The way she stood by you through your rehab, putting up with your foul moods during your recovery." Mom sighed, shaking her head. "I can still see her at six years old, her hair soaked after you squirted her with the garden hose, standing there, her little hands clenched in a fury, calling you the ugliest boy God ever made. Jake, girls, don't get that angry about boys they don't care about."

"Was I really that blind all these years? How could I have not seen it?"

"Don't be too hard on yourself. Impaired optics is part of being young."

"I've been a fool, and now it's too late." The gleam slipped from Jake's eyes, and his shoulders sagged.

"Is it really? I guess you still haven't outgrown your foolishness." Mom had that tone again.

"Mom. She's getting married in less than a week. What am I supposed to do, go to her apartment and tell her I've been a blind fool? Tell her I love her and want to spend the rest of my life with her?"

"That would be a good start, but you don't have to go to her apartment. I noticed her car parked in front of the Fuentes's house." Mom smiled, somehow very pleased with herself, like she'd played some kind of trick on Jake.

"You . . . you set me up. You let me ramble on about my feelings, all the while knowing Maria was four doors away."

Mom's smile grew. She stood up and handed Jake my leash. My tail whipped in excitement. We were going for a walk, but might this one be special? Mom and Jake had talked about Maria, and my nose told me she was nearby.

Jake signaled for me to sit, and I waited impatiently, my tail racing across the floor while Jake clipped the leash to my collar. He accepted a kiss from his mother, and we walked out the door together. Mom stood in the light of the doorway and smiled, watching us turn toward Maria's house.

The Talk

My paws flew across the sidewalk, like when I was a pup, Jake matching me stride for stride. But then a powerful tug pulled me back. I could go no farther. We stood in the darkness in front of the small gate to Maria's house, looking in the window at the soft glow of light surrounding Maria. She sat with her back to us, but I could hear laughter as she played some kind of family game with Diego and her father. My tail thumping, I waited for Jake to take those final steps to the front door to knock and ask Maria to join us. But he didn't move. Instead, Jake sighed and tugged my leash. Shaking his head and mumbling to himself, Jake led me away from Maria's house. But I continued to look back, confused.

We reached the corner, and Jake tugged at my leash again, signaling me to cross over to the park. But I squared my shoulders and sat looking up at him. Something was terribly wrong. Why were we walking away from Maria's house while the joy of her laughter still floated in the air? Jake was foolish to turn away.

I always felt linked to Jake. All the games we

played when younger taught me to trust him completely. Jake never let me down, always knowing what was best. We moved without words or gestures on walks, understanding each other's desires and moving together without thought. But now, standing on the corner waiting for cars to pass before walking farther from where we belonged, I didn't understand. Jake was going the wrong way and making a big mistake.

I stood up and broke free from Jake's loose grasp. With the leash trailing behind me, I raced back to Maria's house. I pushed through the front gate, ran up her walk, and with my front paws in the air, landed on her door with a powerful thud. I scratched at the door madly until it swung open with a whoosh.

"Heavens, Bull. Are you alone? Oh . . . I see you had a mind of your own. Hello, Jake. It seems you two had a difference of opinion on your walk."

After Maria's initial cheerful greeting, she slipped into an uncomfortable silence, matching Jake's. Maria stood in the doorway, shifting from one foot to the other until her father's voice broke the uneasiness.

"Let's call it a game. Diego had us both beaten. Maria, why don't you join Jake? Diego and I have a sink full of dishes that won't wash themselves."

"I win, I win! Maria's walkin' with Jake. I win!" Diego's smile matched his excited voice. Was he joining us on our walk? No. His smile grew, and he pushed the apprehensive Maria out the door before turning his back on us, continuing to shout, "I win! I win!"

The door closed behind us, and my two best friends walked away from the house, neither speaking. We moved toward the park, filled with so many wonderful memories of our times together, but the tension grew with each silent step. Both acted like this was the first walk they'd ever taken together, neither seeming to know what to say or do.

Once more, I saw how strange humans could be. Old friends, walking side by side in uncomfortable silence, forgetting how to play. What was wrong with them?

We crossed the street to the park. I brushed my flank against both of my friends, but no one reached down to touch me. Something troubled them, something I couldn't understand. I had to do something to remind Jake and Maria of things they'd forgotten.

Jake still held my leash loosely, like he had since he trained me as a pup, always confident a quick redirect could get me to stop, start, or turn in any direction he wanted. So again, that night, I easily broke from Jake's grasp. I bolted, running across the street, through the gates, and into the park.

"Bull, get back here!" Jake's surprised voice called out.

But more importantly, I heard the pounding feet of my two friends running side by side into the park to catch me.

"Bull, come here! What's with you tonight?"

My Boy's voice echoed his frustration, but I couldn't obey, not tonight. Jake and Maria had to remember how to play and why they were friends. So I ran in long, loping strides deep into the park before turning to face them. I dropped into a crouch and offered a playful growl. With my head almost on the ground, my butt and tail held high, my eyes shifted from Jake to Maria. I barked, my best big boy bark, daring them to catch me.

Jake hesitated, perhaps still angry and confused by my actions, but Maria smiled. She understood my challenge and shouted out, "All right, the big fella wants to play!"

Then, with a familiar giggle and an emphatic leap, she reached out to grab me. I felt the leash grow tight, but then I was free again. Maria's momentary grasp released.

The wise Maria didn't want the game to end too soon.

Then a bright smile crossed Jake's face. He understood too. Abandoning any attempt to make me heel, my old friends threw all their energies into chasing me around the park, neither trying overly hard to grab hold of my daggling leash. On and on, we ran like when we were young until, exhausted, we fell to the ground high on the hillside under the giant trees.

I panted for air under the soft moonlight until, at last, Jake began to talk.

"I needed that."

"Me too."

"Bull knew. I don't know how, but he did. I was afraid to knock on your door and didn't know how to say what I have to say. But he understood I needed help, and like always, he was there for me."

Maria had been lying on her back, staring up at the flickering night sky, but sat up, a frightened look in her eyes, and turned to face Jake.

"All right, Jake. And what exactly is it you have to say?"

Jake paused and stared at his tightly clasped hands, as if afraid to look up. I nuzzled against him, and he reached out to take Maria's hands. Their eyes met, and he smiled. Jake had found what he'd been searching for.

"Okay, here goes. I love you, Maria. I have for years. I think, deep down, even in my most self-absorbed teenage years, I always did. But I *know* now. I am helplessly, irrevocably in love with you."

"What? You saw me nearly every day of my life, and now, a week before I plan to marry a really great guy, you come to the conclusion you *love me*?" Maria's voice called out in anger, but I smelled something more. Fear.

Even when Diego was at his most difficult, Maria rarely raised her voice so forcefully anymore. But the loud voices didn't worry me. Instead, I grew oddly relaxed. Together, my friends could do anything, and now, at last, they were talking. I knew it would end well. And wow, did they talk. Some of it was almost yelling as they fired back and forth, often not letting the other finish. But I was content. I trusted that working together, they'd find what had been making them so unhappy and causing them to avoid each other at every opportunity.

"I didn't just decide," Jake said. "It took me a while to finally figure it out, and by the time I did, you were engaged to Stephen, and I felt I needed to respect that."

"Sooo . . . You figured out nearly *two years ago* you were in love with me, did absolutely nothing about it because of some classic Jake DiSpirito sense of honor, and now, a week before my wedding, you've decided to tell me?"

"Something like that." Jake shrugged and offered one of his best smiles. A smile that usually caused others to smile back widely, but it didn't work with Maria. Not this night.

"Ugh!"

"Well?" Jake's smile faded, but his eyes glimmered with hope.

"Well, what, Jake? What did you expect, that I'd throw myself into your arms and offer up my undying love?"

"I don't know what I expected. I just knew I had to tell you and couldn't let you get married without you knowing how I feel."

"Damn you, Jake. Damn you! You have no idea how long I waited to hear you say that. All those years, you acted like I wasn't there, or worse, treated me like one of the guys while you ran around making a fool of yourself with that rich girl from the Hill. All the time, I stood by waiting, hoping, and you didn't even look my way. So now, when you finally do . . . I'm sorry, Jake, it's just too late."

"I'm sorry too, Maria. I really am. I didn't mean to make you cry, and it's true, you stood by me through all that and a lot more. You were by my mother's side when we lost my dad. You were there when I struggled with my recovery, too blind and later too scared to do anything about how I felt. But I'd regret it the rest of my life if I didn't finally get the courage to tell you how I feel."

"You have no right to tell me this now, no right

at all." Maria buried her face in her hands, and long, sad sobs filled the night air. "I hate you, Jake DiSpirito. I really, really hate you!"

Jake reached out and grabbed Maria by the shoulders, forcing her to look at him.

"I know you don't hate me, but what I need to know is, do you still love me? Is the girl who told my mother she was going to marry me one day and give her beautiful grandbabies still inside there?"

"She told you?"

"Yes. Tonight. It seems recently lots of people have been reminding me of what I was going to let slip through my hands."

"I'm sorry, Jake. I did tell your mother that, and I meant it, every word of it, with all my heart. I wanted desperately to marry you and raise a family with you. I stood by for years, waiting till I couldn't wait any longer. I've moved on. I'm going to marry Stephen."

For the first time, Jake's anger rose to match Maria's. "Stephen? He doesn't even like dogs. He's got a *cat*!"

"Oh God. So now you're taking tips for the lovelorn from my brother Diego?"

Maria broke away and disappeared into the shadows, running back toward her house. Jake called out, and her pounding footsteps stopped. She turned to face him, the glimmer of streetlight outlining her trembling body.

"Maria, I'm sorry. That wasn't fair. But I have all these people's voices in my head telling me what I should do. I'm struggling to say the right things. Just answer one question for me, honestly. Then, if you still want me to, I will leave you alone and never bother you again."

Maria sighed, staring at the ground, perhaps, even in the darkness, afraid of what Jake might see in her eyes. Then, with one deep breath, she straightened. Holding herself very still, she looked directly at Jake.

"All right, what?"

Jake stared back, seemingly willing Maria to stay. "My dad told me years ago he knew my mother was the woman he wanted to marry because she was the one person in the world he'd trust to raise his kids if anything ever happened to him. I have never known anyone other than you with whom I'd want to raise kids. Maria Fuentes, who do you want to raise your children with?"

PART VI

Our Life Together

So, Maria came to live with Jake and me in a new house all our own. We didn't live with Mom anymore, but it seemed like we were at our old house visiting her or walking up the street to see Maria's family almost every other day.

We still took the long drive to see the sick people at the hospital and visited Anthony, working at the place Dad took him when he couldn't walk well. Old and young, these people behaved better when I was around, and smiles brightened their faces when I entered a room. Being with me helped them relax and start talking when that's what they needed.

Most days, Jake left for work to do the teaching thing like Mom while Maria put on her uniform, which I heard Jake call "scrubs." Like Doctor Yoshida, Maria helped the people at the hospital because she was so good at it. But unlike Jake, Maria didn't leave at the same time every day, so someone was almost always with me.

Today was my favorite kind of day. We could all be together. Maria and Jake ran around the house, cleaning and preparing lots of food. My tail thumped side to side while I gobbled up a delicious piece of meat Jake had dropped in my dish. Tonight, we'd have a house full of laughing people, eating and enjoying themselves while they spent time with my family at our new home. Sam came around a lot now, bringing his friend Phoebe, and even the twins began to visit, bringing friends with them. The twins' friends were nice enough and always kind to me, but they reminded me of when Skyler came around long ago. It can be hard for a boy to find his forever friend, even when that person was always nearby like Maria had been for Jake. But they were together now. That's all I needed. So I endured the distracting chatter from the twins and their friends, talking fast about everything except what they really thought and felt. Humans are funny sometimes.

Mom came early that night and brought lots of food. And, of course, she still made plenty of time for me. Mom smiled and had big hugs for everyone, but when she thought people weren't looking, her smile faded, and her eyes grew sad. I think Mom missed Dad more than any of us. As I watched how happy Jake and Maria made each other, I understood how sadness could creep into Mom's eyes when she thought of the forever love she had lost.

When she left, Maria promised Mom she'd stop by tomorrow to visit. I think Maria saw Mom's sadness, too, and held her extra hard when she kissed her goodbye that night.

Then the house sat empty, our guests all gone, and just like Mom used to, Maria didn't sit down until all the counters were clean and the food put away. After helping her finish, Jake took me for a quick walk, and we came home to find Maria sleeping on the couch. Jake slipped a blanket over Maria before sitting down to tap away at that thing he kept on his desk. Sometimes, Jake laughed out loud, while other times Jake looked sad. Often, he'd just stared straight ahead, silent, his fingers sitting frozen on the desk.

That night, I followed him into the corner and lay under him, my paws pressing against the wall near the desk while Jake tucked his feet under my body. My eyes fluttered while Jake sat motionless, searching for something he couldn't see.

"How's it going, hon?"

I woke to the sound of Maria's sleep-filled voice. She kissed Jake on the lips before dropping to the ground next to me. She quickly found my favorite spot on the top of my chest, scratching me perfectly.

Jake stopped his tapping and looked at Maria. "Good, I guess. Just don't know where I'm going with all this. It's just a jumble of ideas and my need to get them out. Not sure anything will ever be worth publishing. It's strange thinking anyone would ever pay money to read what I have to say. But ever since I was a kid, I found writing cathartic. I hope I have at least one story worth telling."

"Well, you know I think you write beautifully, and I believe you have many important stories to share."

"You and my mom: you're my two-member fan club. I don't know, though. It just feels like I'm searching for something, and I'm not sure what. Sometimes I think I'm close, but then it slips away and what I end up writing rings hollow. If I feel it, the reader will too."

Maria stopped scratching me and glanced up at Jake with that look she got in her eyes only for My Boy. "That makes sense, but I believe you can do anything you set your mind to. You'll find the story you're looking for."

"Anything? Hum. Let's put that to the test. What if I told you I dreamt I walked on water? And the dream was so real, so detailed. I woke thinking I might just be able to dispel the law of physics, even for a moment, and walk across a pool full of water. What would you say?"

Maria smiled, the look in her eyes even brighter. "Well, I'd say wait till winter comes, and I know you could do it."

"God, I love you."

Jake turned away from his desk and took Maria in his arms. They fell to the ground, rolling under the table next to me, giggling. Delighted by this clear invitation to play, I jumped from one to the other, pulling on their sleeves, happily joining them in my favorite game. Jake wrestled with me across the floor, but he must have been tired because I won far more quickly than usual. Soon Jake picked Maria up and carried her off to the room where they slept, closing the door behind them.

It pleased me to see My Boy so full of joy, and I wondered if he knew what I knew. I had noticed a difference in Maria the last few weeks, and now I could tell. She had a small life inside of her. It was still very early, but it was there.

Would it make them both as happy as it made me?

~ ~ ~ ~

Jake put the special bright blanket on my back and led me to the car. It was time to go to work. I circled him, my tail whipping with excitement when he signaled me to get in. We were going to the hospital with all the sick and hurt people, the same place Jake stayed after he got hurt so badly. Each visit was different, and the people I saw were different too. But each person had a need, one I might be able to help with. Many people had a powerful pain that might never go away, but I'd learned by simply being Jake's Best Boy, I could help many of them feel just a little better.

The hospital felt like home now, and lots of old friends were there whenever we visited. Along with Doctor Yoshida, Maria was often there, too, looking confident in her scrubs as she helped the people. Even Anthony sometimes came to talk to the nervous and frightened people.

We started the day in my favorite place: the rooms where all the children were. Their squeals of laughter set my tail spinning with delight. I had to be patient because some of the children, especially those starting to feel better, could be aggressive in their excitement, reaching out to grab and hug me. Still, I was happy to get a small poke or a less-than-gentle hug because that meant they were truly starting to get healthy again.

Maria found us with the children. After saying

hello to me with a hug and scratches behind my ears, she stood up to speak in hushed tones with Jake.

"Eighty-seven years old with congestive heart failure . . . last rites performed, and the family has said their goodbyes... had dogs since she was a little girl. She doesn't have long."

Jake grew still, and I brushed along his leg with my flank. We had a difficult job to do. We left the children and traveled to a different part of the hospital, where the familiar smells of sickness and fear made me pause. Jake stopped and knelt to give me a reassuring hug before leading us forward.

We came to a room where an old woman lay with tubes in her arm and a clear mask over her face. Another woman, a younger version of the old one, sat on the side of the bed, speaking softly and gently stroking the sick woman's long white hair.

If the older woman heard or understood, it didn't show. She lay motionless, the only sound the beeping of a machine and her unsteady struggle to breathe. Jake turned and whispered to a man standing by the door, who nodded and went to the bedside as well. The man brushed the back of his hand across the old woman's cheek and, with a sigh, leaned down to hug the younger one. Sadness flowed out of them as they stepped away, stoop-shouldered and shaking, to sit in nearby chairs.

With my tail held low, I walked to the side of the bed, my nails clicking across the hard, cool floor. I stopped a moment to look up at Jake, his eyes wet. He ran his strong, reassuring hand across my side, and I lay my head on the bed next to the women's hand and waited. I stayed like that for a long time, with nothing happening except for the sound of the old woman's erratic breathing. My eyes flickered, waiting patiently. I'd learned just being there was sometimes enough, but then the old women stirred.

Fingers fluttered, and soon her entire hand slowly moved to find the scruff of my neck. Her hand traveled up purposely to scratch behind my ear, coming to rest on the top of my head. With her first touch, I could tell she'd known dogs and understood us. Her ancient hand was confident and kind. She tried to speak, paused to run her fingers across the back of my neck softly. Then she tried again.

"Oh, you remind me of Ginger. The same soulful eyes. I'll be seeing her soon. We'll be together . . . and young again."

The old woman stopped. Perhaps after a long, full life, she'd left nothing unsaid. She took several short, quick breaths and was gone. I couldn't say where, but the life that was the gentle old woman no longer filled the room. The younger woman cried out with painful sobs as the man, unsteady in his own grief, reached out to console her.

The old woman was gone, and there was nothing more I could do to help. I stepped away and walked over to sit by the younger woman. She dropped to her knees, wrapping her arms around me, and gasped for breath, struggling with her sadness. In time, her breathing steadied, and she began to speak.

"She called you Ginger. That was her dog when she was a little girl. Thank you for coming back to her at the end. It made leaving just a little easier. At least it did for me."

As the woman spoke, I thought of Dad. Like the old woman, Dad was gone too. Sadly, unlike her family, I didn't get to say goodbye. But feeling the gentle touch of the young woman, so much like the older, and listening to the similar tone, I understood part of the old woman endured, just like Dad remained with me. Every time Jake smiled his crooked smile or walked with his shoulders squared and leaning forward, I knew Dad had never left us. He was everywhere, but lately, I sensed something else. I'd begun to feel Dad more and more. Each day now, I could hear his powerful voice in the wind, high on a hillside, calling out to me.

Friends

Maria's belly grew bigger each day. It wouldn't be long now. She moved slower around the house and tired more easily, but I rested contently, watching her and Jake together. Things were different now. When they were young, they could talk and talk, never understanding the other. Now they said so much without making a sound. Long ago, they'd get so angry with each other they couldn't speak, but now, they moved together gracefully, like the wings of a bird as it soared in the sky. They'd glide through all the activities that came their way. They laughed, relishing being alone with each other, but would just as often delight in having guests over to eat, play games, or join us while we simply enjoyed being together.

Sam visited with his friend Phoebe a lot. They had become forever friends, like Jake and Maria. It was funny watching Sam around Phoebe. Sam had always reminded me of Duke, the old Saint Bernard who lived in the house right next to the park when I was a young pup. Duke would see other dogs heading toward the park, pulling on their leash and yapping at Duke while they passed his house. With the relaxed confidence of most big dogs, Duke might raise an eyebrow, or if he didn't particularly like the look of a dog, offer up a long, deep woof to let the passerby know not to trifle with him. But Duke would soon leisurely drop his big head back down on his front paws to continue enjoying the sun's warmth. As the years passed, I thought of Duke often and always tried to carry myself with the same quiet dignity he had shown me when I was young.

Sam had always acted like that around Jake and his friends. While Dougie might yap away or Diego and the twins might race around him with all their nervous energy, Sam would watch indulgently, only speaking when he felt something significant needed to be said. Around Phoebe, though, Sam had transformed into a young pup himself, laughing all the time and excited by the smallest of things. Now he talked more than in all the time I had known him.

One night, Sam and Phoebe came to dinner. Everyone was relaxed, talking and laughing with the comfort old friends find in spending time together. Words like *baby, doesn't matter,* and *healthy* were repeated throughout the night. Like Maria, Phoebe was carrying a life inside her, and I hoped it would make Sam and Phoebe happy like Jake and Maria. Our guests stayed late into the night, softly talking, enjoying each other's company.

After they left, Jake and Maria went to the kitchen, and together they worked picking up the clutter always left behind when we had a party. I got up, moving a bit stiffly, and walked into the room to be with them. After circling a few times, I dropped to the ground by their feet with a *harrumph* and waited for them to finish. Maria moved slowly as my tail swished across the floor to the sound of her happy voice.

"Great news about Phoebe and the baby. I can't believe the change in Sam. He's like a different person. I've never seen him so happy."

"Yes, it's amazing what the love of a great woman will do for a man. I was afraid Sam might never get over his crush on you."

Maria stopped wiping the big bowl she held in her hand and turned to look at Jake. "What are you talking about?"

"Come on, don't pretend you didn't know. All my friends had huge crushes on you. I think that's why it's taken them so long to find the right one. They compare everyone they meet to you, and they keep falling short."

"Oh, don't be silly. I knew about Dougie, but he had a crush on every girl in the Flats and half the girls on the Hill. But Sam, honestly? I never had a clue. Sam? Really?"

"Really, and for years. You know, he actually threatened me once. Said I'd better wake up or lose you forever."

"Well, he wasn't wrong there. It did take you quite a while to wake up. But seriously, I feel terrible. I never even knew Sam felt that way."

"Don't feel bad. Sam could see, long before me, we were meant for each other. And look at him now. He couldn't be happier." Jake took the big bowl, put it high up on a shelf, and turned to look back at Maria.

"But I'm worried about Dougie. He's changed since the breakup with Jeanie. There's an unhappy nervousness in his energy that was never there before. His old joy for life is missing. He used to find pleasure in the simplest things. Now, there's emptiness behind all the chatter. Watching his friends get on with their lives, go off to college, get married, and start families has affected him. It's like he's wondering if any of that will ever happen for him. He works part-time for the city and lives alone in that tiny apartment. I think, for the first time in his life, he's afraid of what's ahead for him."

Maria frowned. Something Jake said had taken some joy out of the night.

"I see it too. It's a shame. Dougie tried to be something he wasn't to please Jeanie, and now it's like he's lost sight of who he is and what makes him so special. He's pulling away, despite everyone's efforts to include him." Maria rubbed her growing belly. "Even tonight, when I called to invite him, he bowed out. Said he already had plans, but I knew he didn't want to be the fifth wheel. The old Dougie never said no to a free meal surrounded by a captive audience. I keep thinking of your mother. She'd have a pearl of wisdom to put this all into perspective. So, trying to channel my best Anna DiSpirito, I'll say: *Good things happen to good people*. Dougie's a smart guy with a big heart. We just have to be there for him and make sure he's ready when it comes knocking. Something good's out there for Dougie. And with some help from his friends, he'll find his path."

"You are a wise woman. Now, please let me finish up here. Just once, can't you go in the living room, put your feet up, and relax."

"Jake, I'm fine. I cut back on my shifts at the hospital this week, and I'm already going stir-crazy. Staying home with my feet up is not for me. I dragged poor old Bull out into the biting cold for three walks the other day. I promise I won't push myself, but I can't just sit still."

"Okay, I know I can't win with you, but please take advantage of the opportunity to rest up. You'll be needing it once the baby comes."

Jake leaned over, smiled, and kissed Maria, but his voice was tense, his eyes anxiously watching Maria's slow shuffle as she worked in the kitchen. The rest of the night, Jake raced around the house, trying to do things for Maria while she lovingly scolded him, frustrated by the attention. Maria winced and touched her stomach several times when Jake wasn't looking.

It wouldn't be long before everything changed.

A Winter's Storm

Maria stopped going to work and stayed home with me every day. She waddled around the house, happily talking to me while she cleaned and painted the room where Jake used to sit and tap away at his desk. Now, late at night, he tapped away at the table where my family ate. Whenever Maria stopped painting, she'd put on a heavy coat, grab my leash, and we'd go on a long, slow walk.

Then, one morning, everything changed. Maria showed no interest in working on the room, going for a walk, or doing anything around the house, but her uneasiness bubbled over, leaving me panting and anxious.

Despite her Dougie-like energy, Maria had grown to become a remarkably calm and relaxed companion. But today, the scent of her nervousness frightened me. Even with her size and awkward walk, Maria couldn't stay still. So I watched her closely, my ear flat and my tail pulled tightly while Maria spent the day fidgeting, moving from one chair to the next without direction or apparent thought in anything she did.

Late in the afternoon, with Maria's unrest growing, I followed her through the house, making sure she was all right. I brushed against her, letting her know I was there for her, and I warmed to Maria's tender touch when she ran her hand across my back. But her tenseness only worsened while the sky grew black, and our house now sat in darkness except for a few flickering candles.

It had begun snowing earlier in the day, and Maria groaned, struggling to her feet to let me out to do my business. The snow in the backyard was up to my belly and continued to fall heavily, covering my body with a white coating by the time I'd pushed my way to my favorite marking tree. Usually, I'd stay out for a while, roll around on my back, and enjoy the feel of the cool powder, but I was worried about Maria. So I lifted my leg and hurried back.

Maria stood by the door, waiting for me, and with a painful grunt, closed the door. The floor was wet before I stepped in. Water streaked with blood crept toward my paws, and sweat covered Maria's face. My body stiffened. Her eyes looked through me, and she called out in pain, grabbing her stomach. Then, with her back pressed against the wall, she dropped to the ground, crying out.

"God, no. Nine, one, one . . . please. Nooo! No power lines, the battery's dead."

The smell of blood mingled with her fear left me trembling like never before. Her cries of pain grew louder while she rocked back and forth on the floor, her head pitched forward. Maria continued to moan, rocking, her finger poking furiously at that black thing she carried everywhere. She often held it up to her ear and talked. It usually made her happy. But today, Maria only got angrier and more frightened the longer she tapped at it. Then, it fell from her hand, and with a deafening scream, she rolled onto her side, crying out in the darkness. She lay in front of me, moaning, with her body curled up as blood stained her dress.

With my tail between my legs, I stood over Maria, whimpering. I tried to nuzzle her face with my nose, and she looked up and stared at me. Her eyes were empty. She didn't know me. Maria needed help, and no one was there but me. I left her side and ran to the front door, barking furiously, trying to call out for help. I scratched at the door till my nails were broken and bleeding, but I couldn't force it open. If only we still lived with Mom. But in our new home, none of our neighbors knew us well or understood my barks weren't simply the noise of a bored or naughty dog. My howls were a cry for help, but if anyone heard me, they must have thought I was just another lonely dog.

Frantically, I ran from the front door and jumped on the couch that looked out on the snow-covered street. Boys wrapped in thick, warm coats played in front of our house, running back and forth, throwing balls of snow at each other. I barked my deepest warning bark, and one boy stopped under a flickering street light, his face bright and joyful. He looked up at me, his intelligent eyes showing interest, and he stepped toward the house.

But a flash of white flew across the darkening sky, hitting him in the back of the head. The boy yelped and turned quickly, giggling, a broad smile spreading across his face. He bent down, scooped up a handful of snow, and spun away from the house, hurrying to return to his game.

In panic, I jumped down and ran back to Maria, her eyes now closed, and her breathing strained. I didn't know what was wrong, but I needed to find a human. Quickly.

There were humans in the front yard who could help, and I had to get to them.

Running as fast as I could, I jumped onto the couch and crashed out through the window with a shattering explosion. Painful, jagged bits spread around me and flew into the air. I tumbled, rolling over in the thick snow several times, then pounced up to race toward the boys as I barked madly.

They all jumped back, the smell of fear flowing from their young bodies. Finally, the boy who'd seen me in the window appeared from the back of the crowd. Braver than the others, he stepped forward.

"Whoa, buddy. Somethin' wrong? You wouldn't jump through a picture window if somethin' weren't messed up. Zach, I saw a cop car in front of the diner. Get 'em and quick. This guy needs some help."

He spoke softly to me, he wanted to help, but I couldn't tell him it wasn't me who was in trouble. I pulled away from his grasp and ran back to our house. I barked and scratched at the door as the boy ran after me.

"What's wrong, buddy? You just crashed through a window to get outta there. Now you're actin' crazy, tryin' to get back in. Guys, where's

Zach with the cops? Somethin's messed up here, and this dog's gonna need a vet."

"Cops are comin.' I just saw them turn the corner. Careful, Bobby, that dog's crazy."

I continued scratching at the door, trying to get back to Maria, but then I felt the presence of others coming, and the boy called out to them.

"Officer! I don't know what's up, but somethin's wrong. This dog jumped out the front window like the house was on fire and is actin' crazy now tryin' to get back in."

"Hank, call for an ambulance. I looked in through the side window. Someone's passed out on the floor in the kitchen."

A man and woman in uniforms like Dad used to wear had arrived, and the woman started shouting orders. Surely they'd help. I jumped back and forth behind them, barking as they kicked in the door and ran into the house to kneel by Maria's side. Soon more people in different uniforms arrived. They strapped Maria onto a small bed with wheels and pushed it out through the deepening snow to a tall, long car with bright flashing lights on top. I ran alongside, barking, and tried to jump in the car with Maria, but the woman in the uniform grabbed my collar to hold me back.

"It's all right, big guy. You did a good thing, a real good thing. Good boy. We're going to get her some help."

I whimpered, watching the car drive off with its lights flashing and loud noises flowing from it until I lost it in the swirling snow and dark night. But I stopped pulling. This woman had one of those voices some humans have that make a dog trust they know what's best. So I stood silently while she continued to talk.

"Now, let's take care of you. My partner just called your dad. He's going to the hospital, but he called a friend who'll be here any minute. He'll take you to the vet. You be a good boy, and let me check you out while we wait. Hank, radio dispatch and tell them we'll be here just a bit longer."

"Come on, Claire. It's just a friggin' dog. Let's leave it for animal rescue."

"Damn it, Hank. Just do it."

I relaxed. The woman was a good human, and she was in charge. I could tell by her smell and the way she handled me the women had dogs of her own. She mentioned Dad, so I figured she must have known him, which helped me calm down. The woman took me back into the house, and I lay by the broken front door while she cleaned my cuts and wrapped my wounds in cloth. She worked carefully with each movement of her hands, continuing to speak calmly to me. Her partner tried to talk to her one more time, but she muzzled him with a hard stare. He shook his head and walked back in silence to sit in their car.

The nice woman had just finished bandaging my paw when a truck with big wheels and a giant blade on its front pulled up to our house. I lifted my head to see Dougie jump out with an unusual frown on his face. He mumbled, walking toward us, and I stood up in the open doorway to greet him, my tail wagging.

"My best payday of the year. The town's payin'

big money, which says nothin' for the side jobs the town doesn't know about. I shoulda called Sam to get here in that ridiculous Fiat of his. What's he think he's gonna do once the baby gets here?"

Dougie rambled on, staring up at the falling snow, and didn't see me at first, then he stopped, his eyes opening wide.

"Oh, jeez. Bull, what happened?"

"Are you Douglas Donovan?" The nice lady turned away from me. She had changed back to her *I'm in charge* voice.

Suddenly, I realized how very tired I felt and dropped back to the ground. Dougie was here. He and the nice lady could handle everything else. At last, I could rest. Humans I trusted stood over me.

"Yeah, I'm Dougie, ah, Douglas Donovan. Got here quick as I could. The roads are a mess. What happened? Jake called, sayin' Maria went into labor unexpectedly and asked me to get over here to check on Bull. He didn't say he was hurt."

"Well, Mr. Donovan, I'm Officer Nguyen. Thanks for getting here quickly. My partner and I should have been out of here by now. A lot's happening with the storm, but I didn't want to leave till someone got here to look after the dog." The nice lady knelt beside me while she talked. "I checked out . . . is it *Bull*? Good name for him. He's in decent shape, considering what he just did. He's got a nasty gash on his front right paw that I managed to bind with a dishtowel while we waited. He'll need some stitches. I didn't find any other severe gashes, but he needs to get checked out."

"Thanks, officer. I'll get him to the vet's

straightaway. Do you know how Maria's doing? And I'm still a little unclear on how exactly Bull got cut up like this."

"Your friend's wife was hemorrhaging. The power lines got knocked down with all the snow, and it looks like the battery on her cell phone went dead. She wasn't in great shape when we first got here, but the EMTs gave her some blood, and her color looked a bit better by the time they got her in the ambulance. They took her to Holy Family. It was the closest. You can check in on her there."

The woman paused, scratching under my chin, then continued talking. "I'm no doctor, but if Bull hadn't smashed out the window to get help, I don't know what would have happened. Damnedest thing I've ever seen. I've been around dogs my whole life. Have two of my own. I only hope one of my dogs loved me enough to do what this guy did. Tell your friend he's got one special dog."

"I will, but they already know. I could tell you stories about this guy." Dougie knelt beside me and joined the nice lady petting me, but he wasn't looking at me while he spoke. "I better get him looked at. Thanks again for all you did, Officer . . . ?"

"Nguyen. Claire Nguyen."

"Thanks again, Officer . . . Claire." Dougie stopped to look around at the shattered window and broken door and picked up a splintered piece of wood. "I better call our buddy Sam to get over here to board up this door and window." Dougie smiled one of his old Dougie smiles and continued talking to himself, retracing the path he made in the snow back to his truck. "Sam drivin' that friggin' Fiat in this snow. That'll be a show."

Dougie was very attentive and gentle as I slowly limped toward his truck, but he kept looking back at the lady who had been so kind to me. She had a bright look in her eyes and smiled back at him before turning to push her way through the high snow toward her car.

My body ached with each step, and Dougie had to help me jump into his truck, but the pain meant nothing. Instead, my thoughts focused on the memory of Maria riding away in the long car, then lost in the blinding snow as its throbbing noise slowly faded to silence.

Was Maria okay? Had I done enough?

Gio

I spent the next few days at Dougie's small place, pacing from room to room, waiting and worried. I had to know: Was Maria okay? Then, one morning, Jake came by with a big grin on his face and gave me one of the longest, most painful hugs ever. He smiled constantly and talked away at Dougie, who sat oddly calm, nodding his head, smiling and listening to Jake, who wouldn't stop hugging me. Based on how Jake acted, I had to believe Maria was okay, but I couldn't be sure. I smelled hints of her on Jake, but were they old? Her scent, mixed with so many other smells, confused me. Without any clear sign of Maria, I continued to patrol the rooms of Dougie's apartment, walking from window to window, waiting for a sign.

Finally, one bright, sunny afternoon, Dougie helped me into his truck. With my nose pressed against the frosty window, we drove through the snowy streets, my tail thumping wildly when he turned onto the road where I lived with Jake and Maria. I ran up the walk, ignoring the pain in my injured paw, and was met at the front door by My

Boy, who'd knelt to greet me. For once, I was more interested in seeing someone else. My nose twitched. Could it be? With my tail flapping wildly and my bottom swinging from side to side, I barked a deep, joyful hello.

Maria sat on the couch, holding a tiny baby. She looked up, smiled, and called to me. I'd been around Baby Gina and other babies before, so I knew I had to be on my Best Boy behavior. Still unable to control my swishing tail, I calmed myself with one last bark and walked carefully toward Maria. Her smile grew, and she called once more. I rested my head in Maria's lap next to the soft, warm baby, my tail settling into a slow, steady swing. Maria gently stroked my neck while I nuzzled against her and the baby.

I was home again.

Dougie, moving cautiously, came over and sat on the couch next to Maria to see the new member of our family. "How you feelin'?"

"Much better, Dougie, thanks. The doctors say if the EMTs hadn't shown up when they did, we would have lost the baby for sure, and I might have...."

"Okay, none of that. You're fine. Our baby's fine, and we have Bull to thank." Jake smiled, but his eyes were tired and red, like when he'd stayed out late with the boys years ago.

"Jake's right. Remember my Dougie Donovon's rules for a happy life, number twenty-seven: *There's no sense talkin' about what might have been.* You and the baby are fine and all because of the big guy with his head in your lap. That female police officer who stayed with Bull till I got there couldn't believe what he'd done. Said she'd never seen anythin' like it. I told her that's cuz she's never met Bull before."

"Officer Nguyen. She stopped in to check on me while I was still at Holy Family. She left her card."

"Hum, that was nice. What, ah . . . did you talk about? I mean, besides the baby." Dougie got up and started pacing back and forth in front of Maria. No longer calm, Dougie suddenly found his old Jack Russell self.

Maria smiled, watching Dougie's anxious movements. "She'd just gotten off duty, so she stayed for quite a while. We talked about how brave Bull was and how both of our families struggled to come to America. You know, her parents were some of the last people to get out of Vietnam after the fall of Saigon." Maria paused, her eyes twinkling like she had a secret. "Oh, yes, I almost forgot. And we talked about you."

Jake let out a short chuckle like Maria had told some joke, and Dougie certainly acted interested.

"Me?"

"Yes, Douglas, you. Now listen. Claire Nguyen appears to be a charming young woman who seemed sincerely interested in checking to see how I was doing. But I believe she had an additional motive for visiting me. So here, Dougie, take the card and give her a call. I think, aside from Bull, she found you one of the more interesting individuals she's met in some time."

Dougie stopped pacing and reached over to take something from the table where Maria had pointed.

He studied it intently, rocking back and forth on his feet, a wide grin spreading across his face.

"Succumbed to the old Dougie Donovan charm, did she? Aw, she couldn't help it. After all, she's only human. I just may have to give Officer Nguyen a call."

"You do that, but remember, be yourself. Claire Nguyen liked you. Don't try to pretend to be someone or something you're not." Maria still smiled, but her voice had changed to the voice she used when she wanted to help keep me safe.

"Got it. Be myself. Hey, what's not to love?"

Dougie's face lit up with his old familiar glow, looking happier than he had been in a long time. He sat back down and watched silently for the rest of the visit while Jake and Maria talked on and fussed with the baby. Dougie nodded his head contentedly, listening to all they said, but he had a far-off look in his eyes, like he was thinking about something important he needed to do.

Soon, Dougie started coming to the house with Claire, the nice lady who'd helped Maria and me the day the baby was born. Claire acted the same around our home as she did that first day. She remained confident and in control without her uniform, but I soon discovered she had a wonderfully serene side. So calm and content with everything around her, I often found myself happily coming to sit by her feet in a crowded room.

Dougie remained energetic as ever. But, amazingly, around Claire, Dougie had become a slightly different, even happier version of his old self. Dougie could still talk nonstop as everyone around him giggled or groaned. But now, he could just as easily sit silently for long periods, listening to other people's conversations, often speaking only to encourage Claire to tell a story. She'd talk in her soft, kind voice, with Dougie's smiling encouragement and then roaring in laughter as the gentlewoman's story ended.

The change in Dougie made me think of the many young pups I had known who never stopped yapping. In time, the pups learned they were loved and grew content, no longer needing to call out for attention like they had when they were young. The old Dougie still appeared, usually with some prodding from Sam or Jake. His familiar energy was still clearly there as Dougie bounced with those old rapid movements, telling a story, finishing with his famous body-shaking laughter. It seemed no one found more delight in his stories than Claire. Dougie would reach out to take her hand, and she'd smile at his latest tale. Then, with his head resting on her shoulder, Dougie would sit back contentedly, silent again, listening to others now take their turn telling stories.

~ ~ ~ ~

The baby's name was Giovanni, and everyone called him Gio. But occasionally, I heard Jake call him John, which pleased me most of all. In the early days, the only thing the little one did was cry, eat, and sleep. So, content, I'd drift off to sleep at Maria's feet with the baby nursing as faded memories of being nurtured by my mother hovered over me.

Then, with flickering eyes, those all-but-forgotten times rushed back, carrying memories of being a young pup, safe and warm with a mother who'd sacrifice anything to protect me.

The days passed, one to the next, and Gio grew bigger. In no time, he was crawling and then just as quickly walking, tottering around the room, using anything he could find to keep himself from falling over. Often that thing seemed to be me. He'd grab hold of my ear or pull at my tail. Sometimes it hurt, but he was just a human puppy learning. I had to be gentle and watchful with him. Everyone laughed when he grabbed for my ear, only to find the nub of my tattered stump. He swiftly toppled over. But with a personality much like his father's, he bounced up quickly, smiling and looking for his next adventure. Gio soon learned my undamaged ear and my tail were the best things to reach for when in danger of falling, and he'd grab hold, following me everywhere on our walks through the house.

I didn't run quite like I used to, but I still delighted in playing with Gio, chasing him around the floor and watching him squeal with joy. Gio would chase me around the house, laughing joyfully, trying to recapture a ball I'd stolen from him. I enjoyed all of this, but my greatest pleasure was having the young boy curl up beside me in the sunlight of the front window. Lying on my side, with Gio's head resting against my belly, we'd slip off together into a deep and restful sleep.

One afternoon, Mom stopped by to visit, waking Gio and me from a long nap. With Baby Gio around, Mom spent a little less time with me, but the baby brought my family such pleasure, I was content watching everyone fuss over him. After a fun meal, where Gio managed to drop lots of food on the floor for me to gobble up, the house grew quiet. Maria carried Gio off to bed, leaving Mom alone to talk with Jake.

"How's the writing coming?"

"Oh, I don't know, Mom. I teach all day, come home, grade papers, play with John a bit, and help Maria around the house. By then, I'm exhausted. I've got a few stories I've started, but there's nothing that's driving me. Nothing seems to resonate with the fullness I'm searching for. I talked to Maria about it a few weeks ago. It's been a struggle finding a story to wrap myself around."

Mom reached across the table, touching Jake's face like when he was a boy. "If your father were here, he'd tell you, 'If it were easy, everybody would do it.' Sorry, hon, but you know it's true. I've read what you've shared with me, and I think you write beautifully. There's an insightfulness and appreciation for life that you capture wonderfully. You have to keep working and growing. You'll find your true voice."

"You see it too, though. Something is missing. Sometimes I feel like someone else is doing the writing. What I write doesn't resonate as real and true. I feel like I'm writing around the story and not living it."

"Hon, you know I can't give you any professional advice, but I'll offer one thought. Write about what you know. Find something you feel passionate about, and write that story."

Jake smiled and pointed his finger at Mom. "Something tells me this is the same advice you give your third graders when they have to pick a science project but, coincidentally, it applies to me. I just have to figure out how to get there."

"Jake, you are an amazing young man, a loving husband, and father, with an appreciation for the beauty in life. It may take time to find the story meant for you to tell, but I know you will, and it will be a story worth telling."

"I hope you're right."

Jake stood up, gave Mom a big hug, and turned away to take dishes from the table. When Mom couldn't see, his smile faded, and his eyes clouded over. Despite all the joy in his life with Mom, Maria, and Baby Gio, Jake still searched for something more. I didn't know how, but I wanted to help My Boy find his way.

Second Time Around

Maria went back to work, and Gio and I started spending time with Mom at our old house. Like me, Mom didn't move as fast as she used to, but that wasn't the biggest change in Mom. Around other people, Mom was still the strong and kind woman we all loved so much. But when she was alone, and no one could see, she'd lower her head and cry. Looking at and playing with Gio could fill Mom with such joy. But sometimes, this could bring heartbreaking sobs, and she'd pick up a confused Gio and hold him tightly to her chest.

Mom saw it too. Gio looked just like Dad. We all missed him, but it was clear Mom felt the pain the deepest. Despite all the joy our family brought, she had never wholly recovered from the loss of Dad. I'd brush against her and feel her gentle touch. I wanted Mom to know I would do all I could to help her find the way back to a happier place. Humans seem to hold onto pain longer than dogs do and sometimes need our help as they struggle to move on.

Slowly, our lives moved forward, one day into

the next. Then, before I knew it, Maria had another baby inside her, and once again, we all waited, watching her grow bigger.

It wasn't long before she stayed home every day to take Gio and me on long, slow walks. I tired easier now, but we didn't move quickly between Gio's short, choppy steps and Maria's increased size. I still enjoyed being out. The weather grew warm, and Maria often took a thick blanket and food so we could sit on the grass in the park to watch Gio play with the other children.

"How'd you do today?"

We'd returned from the park late one afternoon, and Jake greeted us at the door. He picked up Gio and raised him high over his head, spinning him as the boy shouted with glee. But Jake's eyes lingered on Maria, who had grown bigger with each passing day.

Maria smiled and dropped onto the couch by the window with a heavy grunt.

"Good. Everything's easier the second time around, and I'm wiser. So I'm taking advantage of my free time. We spent the afternoon at the playground on Washington Ave. It's a bit of a haul, but Gio marches like a trooper, and Bull does fine. I just have to remember not to push the pace."

Jake sat down next to Maria, tickling Gio, who he held in his lap, and Jake's face grew serious.

"Yep, our old warhorse is pretty amazing. Hard to believe he'll be fifteen in a few months."

Maria leaned over to take Gio from Jake and rested the boy on her knee. "I know. Seems like just yesterday I saw you carrying this little ball of fur under your winter coat, knocking on every door on the street because you wanted to show him off to the entire neighborhood. You were so proud, and I was so jealous. I swear, it wasn't you I liked back then. I came over to your house all the time because Bull had captured my heart."

Jake nodded. "Tell yourself whatever you need to. I won't even argue the point. Dougie always said Bull's the best wingman out there, and I'd be a fool not to realize how much I owe him. He risked his life for me on that mountain and stayed by my side through my recovery. Almost breaking down your door that day when I didn't dare knock. . . . what he did the day John was born. . . . I don't know what I'll do when the time . . ."

Jake's eyes grew wet, and Maria shifted on the couch to bring her and Baby Gio closer to him while she spoke.

"Try not to think about that. Every day is a gift. Bull's doing well and enjoying himself. So let's be grateful for each day we have with him."

I lifted my head and looked up. I wanted to get up on the couch and join them, but getting up was harder than it used to be. So I watched Maria hug Jake, and my tail swished softly across the floor. I knew she was helping My Boy.

Gio saw the attention given to his father and squirmed around in his mother's lap to wrap his arms around Jake too. Finally, Jake's sadness faded, and with a broad smile on his face, he gave Gio back to Maria and lowered himself to the ground next to me.

"This family moment isn't quite complete." Jake

gave me a powerful hug like he did when he was a boy. Then he reached under my belly, carefully lifted me by my haunches, and brought me to my feet to help boost me onto the couch with the others.

"That's it, buddy. Let's rest on the couch with the rest of the family." Jake paused a moment and held me tight as he continued. "We've come a long way together, you and I. You gave me a big scare that first Christmas when we left you alone, and you almost destroyed the house. I was afraid Mom and Dad might not be patient enough, but I knew you were special from the first moment I looked into your eyes."

The sun sat low in the sky, but the light still streaked through the window, and I wiggled closer before dropping my head in Maria's lap. Baby Gio crawled over, rubbed his eyes, and curled up against me, wrapping his arms around my neck.

With hushed baby breaths, Gio slowly fell asleep while Jake lowered himself to the floor in front of us. He leaned back against the couch, resting his head on my chest. Jake draped one arm across Maria's knee and reached back to rest his other hand on the slumbering Gio. Then Jake's breathing changed, the softening glow of the early evening lulling him to join us in sleep.

I woke to the sound of Jake's voice and the bustling activity of him and Maria scurrying around the house.

"Mom, can you get over here quickly? Maria thinks it's time. Yeah, okay, thanks . . . Thanks. Her bag is packed. We'll get out of here soon as you get here. Hurry. Please."

Jake dropped a bag by the door while Maria paced back and forth across the small room with her hands on her back. Breathing heavily, Maria raised her hands to her stomach and cried out. Her time had come.

A New Life

Mom arrived, soon followed by an excited Papa Tomás, whom Jake now called Abuelo. Humans, with all their names. I never could make sense of them all, but greater events were happening for me to concern myself with than the names people used for the ones they loved. Mom walked behind Jake, carrying a small bag. He looked straight ahead, moving carefully, as he led Maria to the car. Papa Tomás stood in the house's doorway with Gio in one arm, grasping my collar firmly with his other hand. He whispered kind words but was wise to hold me tight because I'm not sure how good a boy I would have been if kindly Papa Tomás didn't have such a tight grasp of my collar. Although I wanted to break free and follow Jake and Maria, I knew that wasn't what Jake would want. So I stood listening to Papa Tomás's gentle voice as Mom, anxiously smiling, turned away from the car to walk back to us.

They were gone for several days, leaving Gio and me to stay with Mom. Abuelo Tomás often came to help Mom with Gio, and it pleased me to see the light back in her eyes as she watched Abuelo Tomás carry a squealing Gio on his shoulders around the house.

I stayed at Mom's for several days, and everyone was happy, which helped me relax. I could smell Jake and Maria's scent on the others each time they came back from leaving me alone, so I knew they were safe. Still, I wanted Maria and Jake back with us. After several anxious days, they reappeared with another tiny human they called Paloma.

Like most humans, Paloma had several names, but her most common name seemed to be *a handful*. I discovered, like grown-ups, baby humans were all different. Baby Gio almost never cried, and if he did, it was because he was hungry or had somehow hurt himself. But Baby Paloma cried all the time. Morning, noon, and night. She cried with a full belly or an empty one after a long nap or when it felt like it was time for another. She seemed to cry like some dogs bark just because they can.

When happy, she was joyful, but in the early days, those moments were few. She slept little, and neither did anyone else in the house. It seemed Baby Paloma wanted everyone to know she had arrived, and we did. Fortunately for everyone in our home, the one place Baby Paloma grew quiet was by my side. When Paloma was very tiny, Maria placed the baby in a little pod they carried from place to place. When the baby was particularly cranky, they'd set the pod on the floor, and I'd curl up beside it with my nose resting inside next to her. Paloma's breathing would grow steadier upon seeing me, and her crying slowly stopped. Sometimes she'd fall asleep while running her tiny hands across my face as she learned the pleasures of petting a dog. But whatever the situation, the family soon learned it was best to have me nearby if they wanted a peaceful house.

In time, the baby was large enough that Maria didn't put her in the pod all the time. Instead, Maria placed a fluffy blanket on the floor in a sunny spot of the house so Paloma and I could sleep side by side, enjoying the sun and the warmth of each other's bodies. Sometimes Gio joined us in a nap, but he was generally much too busy a young boy to sleep, and he'd run off, searching for a new game to play. Occasionally, he'd stop from all the frantic movement to come over to where Paloma and I lay to give us both long wet kisses before hurrying away to find more excitement.

Then one day, despite all the distractions, noise, and lack of sleep, Jake and Maria began bustling with a familiar old activity. My family was planning another party. Maria cooked every free moment she had, and many old friends stopped by, dropping off more food while, of course, making time for special hellos with Gio, Paloma, and me.

I lay on a blanket in the sun, resting with Paloma by my side. Gio gave us both a quick hug and sloppy kisses, but filled with his usual joyful energy, he didn't linger. He was gone in a blur, chasing the ball he threw from room to room, barely slowing to accept a kiss from Mom, who'd stopped by to help Maria. With Gio gone, I rested for a moment, and the room grew quiet but for the sound of Mom's loving voice.

"I have the whole morning off, so take advantage of my time. Let me help you get those serving trays out of the attic and set up the tables for tomorrow."

"I hate putting you out, but I can use the help. I'm flat-out with the kids, and there's so much to do. We should have christened the baby months ago, but we've been so busy and wanted to wait until Tommy and Karen could get the time off to travel up from Florida with your parents."

"First of all, my darling daughter, you are not putting me out. I want to help. And secondly, thank you for scheduling so my parents could come. They've slowed down, and I don't know how many more trips they'll be able to make. But I didn't want them to miss this. So please, put me to work."

"Yes, ma'am, but first answer a question. How are *you*... really?"

Mom stopped and smiled an old familiar smile. "Better. I still think of John every day. I always will, but life goes on, and I have family who needs me. Life is good and getting better each day. Now, let's get to work."

For the rest of the morning, Mom and Maria rushed around our home, cooking, covering tables with cloths, and pushing chairs into all corners of the house. Mom left, but Diego came and continued helping move big boxes and chairs to places Maria wanted. Paloma began to wail with one of those long, seemingly never-ending painful cries. And Maria, looking exhausted, took her into the dark sleeping room to feed while Diego continued moving boxes.

"Okay, Bull, my old friend, Tío Diego has gotta

go. Tell Maria I hadda get the four fifteen bus, but I'm gonna see you all tomorrow."

Diego hugged me and was gone, but the door didn't close all the way when he left.

Baby Paloma's wailing slowly faded, replaced by the buzz of Gio, awake from his nap, now chasing his ball into the front room. Full of energy and curiosity and alert to any changes in the small world surrounding him, Gio wasn't different from the young puppies I'd known. It wasn't long before Gio noticed the door hadn't completely closed and hurried over to explore his potentially expanding view of the world. I gave a warning bark, but Gio, much too curious, turned away. He pushed the door open in no time, threw his ball far out into the street, and set off out of the house after it.

I often struggled now getting up and tended to stay where I was once I'd found a comfortable spot, but not today. I jumped up in an instant and ran out the door, barking at Gio and running after him.

Gio turned to look back and smiled, running faster, thinking we were playing one of the chase games he enjoyed so much. But he didn't see the danger in the busy street ahead. With a series of anxious bounds, I landed on top of Gio, knocking him to the ground. I hovered over him, barking madly while he giggled, thinking our game had continued. I held Gio like I would a playful young pup, pinned beneath me, ignoring the painful sound of screeching tires and the frustrated yells of the people in their cars.

Maria burst out of the door, holding Paloma to her hip. Her eyes lit with fear and tears, Maria ran into the noisy street.

~ ~ ~ ~

"I feel like such a terrible mother. I was exhausted, and Paloma hadn't napped all morning. I took her to nurse and fell asleep with her next to me. I've got no excuse. What would have happened if Bull wasn't there to stop John from running farther into the street? You should have seen Bull standing over him, refusing to let him move. But I feel horrible. How could I let it happen?"

I lay at Maria's feet while she held the fussing Paloma in her arms. Despite the excitement of family and friends filling our yard, Maria's face lacked its usual smile, and our friends took turns trying to help. She sat at a large picnic table, surrounded by the friends we'd made through the years. Anthony and Camille, Sam and Phoebe, and now Dougie and Claire. They all had a baby in their lap or were getting up frequently to check on an older child running around our yard with Our Boy Gio, who raced everywhere, playing the latest energy-filled, noisy game he'd created. Gio hurried over to kiss the baby and offer me a warm embrace before disappearing again in a blur.

"You're human. It could have happened to anyone."

"Camille's right. I remember what it was like before Simone got over the colic. We were flat-out, and we didn't have a three-year-old running us ragged at the same time."

"I try to tell myself the same thing but still feel

terrible. I just thank God for Bull." Maria paused, her voice growing soft. "I caught Jake crying the other day when he got back from a short walk with Bull. We can see he's fading, but yesterday is proof of how much we still need him."

Jake came by, kissed Maria, scratched under my chin, and took Paloma in his arms before hurrying off to follow the bustling Gio around our small yard.

Dougie reached down and scratched behind my ear. "It's amazing how important Bull's been in all our lives, through so many good times and some pretty tough ones. I never would've met Claire without him. Bull's been the most loyal friend any of us could ever ask for."

Like so many people I loved, Dougie had changed. Anthony no longer struggled, sad or anxious, and Sam laughed like he never had when he was younger. Although still filled with an amazing joy for life, Dougie had also grown. He now had relaxed confidence flowing from him that brought a smile to everyone's faces, even more than his constant chatter had so long ago.

But most of all, the changes in Maria and Jake pleased me the most. My best friends, who'd spent so much time when they were young talking but never understanding each other, not seeing the things right in front of them, had transformed. Maria had grown into a beautiful, strong woman who reminded me more each day of only one person: Jake and my wonderful mom. While Jake, the kind and gentle boy I had loved all my life, had grown to be the most admirable of men. Surrounded by friends and family, I watched him with pleasure, a loving father who would have made his own now long-gone father very proud. Yes, Dad was gone, but with each passing day, rather than slipping further away, I found myself remembering him ever more clearly. At night, as sleep beckoned, I could almost hear Dad's voice calling to me from high on a hillside, pulling me back, back to the love and job we had shared.

I rested my head in Maria's lap, and my eyes fluttered as I stirred again to her gentle touch. Then, the clatter around me softened, and I slipped off to sleep while the noise-filled party continued around me.

But the call drawing me away from the ones I love grew stronger with each setting sun.

The Calling

I'm so very tired. Jake had to help me stand up the last few days, placing his strong hands around my waist to keep me up while I limped to the backyard to do my business. I don't linger to sniff and explore as I did in the past, only shuffle back into the house before dropping down to the floor with an achy groan.

Today, I don't want to get up at all.

Jake looks small, smaller than I've ever seen him. Maria's crying. Little Gio is sad, and even young Paloma is solemn, taking her short, choppy steps around the house while she keeps repeating, "Best dog ever. . . . Best dog ever."

It's time for me to go. It's time for me . . . to let go. I don't know where I'm going, but it's time to sleep.

A kind lady has come to our house. She's attaching a tube to my paw like Jake had when he was hurt so badly. But this is different.

My family has come to say goodbye. I rest my head in Maria's lap, and Jake gently caresses my stubby ear, mangled so long ago when I battled the giant. I sigh, knowing Jake is thinking of that day too.

Abuelo Tomás, his eyes filled with tears, gives Mom a long embrace, and my tail slowly swishes. I've seen Mom and Abuelo Tomás growing closer, dimming the sadness haunting them, and I hope they can help each other find more happiness in their lives. Then, with tears falling faster, he takes the children by the hand and leads them away.

Mom comes to kneel next to Jake, and he puts his arm around her. I stir to Mom's touch as she softly runs her hand across my back.

"My furry godsend, you saved my life. You saved my son and grandson. You saved this family. We can never pay you back for all you've done, for all you've meant to us. Travel well, my old friend, and wherever you go, we will be with you. Always."

Mom slowly rises and turns away, her body trembling. I fight to keep from drifting off as Jake's face now hovers over me. I lift my head toward him, unwilling to leave. I lick his face like I did the day we met. He tastes the same as all those years ago, healthy and gentle, with the inner strength that drew me to him. My eyes are heavy, and the noise around me fades. I feel the tender caress of the people I have loved for all these years, and then this, too fades. The last thing I hear is Jake's choked voice.

"Goodbye, my Best Boy."

I close my eyes. My last thought . . . *Have I done enough*?

I'm filled with an incredible feeling of lightness.

I'm floating, drifting, high up, away from those I love. Jake is crying in Maria's arms as I struggle to stay, but the pull is too strong. Something calls out to me lovingly, and I must follow. Gently, I'm swallowed up: floating, pain-free.

Memories of my life with my family flash before my eyes, like trees seen from a speeding car. It's all there—the pain, the joy, the love that will endure through time. I let go of the last string to this special life I led, now knowing My Boy will be fine.

I'm at peace.

Far off, a dot of light flickers, and I continue drifting toward it. My eyes follow the dot, the only glimmer in an otherwise empty world, and I feel a warmth. Suddenly, another light appears, then another, leaving a trail to follow. Soon, my world is aglow with boundless dancing lights, like the sky on a clear winter's night. The lights multiply until they meld into one giant sun that explodes. I close my eyes to a blinding whiteness. I feel safe and loved.

When I open my eyes, I'm standing high on a sunlit hillside. A summer's sun warms my body.

A woman walks ahead of me, a young child straddling her hip. The woman has a sack on her shoulder filled with wild berries and roots. She stops by a bush, her hands quick and knowing, adding more berries to her sack. In the distance, a man, powerful and lean, surrounded by sunlight, calls out to me. He's holding a long, sharp stick, leading others as we travel through forests and open fields, hunting for our next meal.

Our gaze meets, and I look into those familiar eyes. Hard and demanding, they carry the fire of someone willing to sacrifice everything for the ones they love. Then, with his stick, he points off to the slope of another hill in the distance. My nose twitches, and I raise my head. A boy, young and confident, is roaming away, too far from our pack.

A warm breeze caresses my face, and I remember my dream by the campfire with Jake and Dad, the dream I could never understand. And now I do.

I am back with the first boy. I bark a tender warning and run toward the boy. I'm young and strong, as strong as I've ever been. I fly to the boy with powerful strides, both ears pinned against my head. The boy sees and turns toward me, his arms open wide, his bright face filled with a joyful smile.

He looks like Jake.

He looks like so many I've loved.

He drops to the ground as the man calls out to me. We are partners, and the boy is our life. We each have a job to do.

Racing, I move ever closer to him.

My Boy.

I am home again.

Epilogue: The Circle Continues

Jake walked with a purpose back in his step. That all-too-familiar bounce had been missing for more than six months, replaced by sadness and pain. He had lost a friend. No, not a friend, his best friend. A friend who had meant more to him than words could describe. And the void left behind was immeasurable.

He had moved through his days with a burden that wouldn't abate. Going to work each day, Jake stood in front of classrooms full of bright-eyed, occasionally eager high school students, trying to inspire them to the beauty and provocation of the written word.

He'd speak of poets like Butler, Keats, Frost, and Dickinson; authors like Steinbeck, Hemingway, Orwell, and Rand; and philosophers like Aristotle, Thoreau, and Nietzsche. Men and women with broad and eclectic views on life, morality, and the human experience. Ideas he could usually wrap his mind and energies around as he sought to inspire the students to question, explore, debate, and study. But for months now, Jake felt he'd been failing. He remained the oh-so-demanding but ever-popular Mr. D, with students who took his assignments home over a long weekend if no others. But Jake's soul wasn't immersed in his time with the students, and he feared he'd been failing them, failing himself.

Life at home had faired only slightly better. Each night, he and Maria still organized evening dinners where they'd sit around the kitchen table with their two small children, talking about their days and sharing their accomplishments. The children, barely four and two, had already learned to relish these moments, knowing this was their time when no phones, computers, or televisions were allowed to penetrate this cherished family time together. Here too, Jake feared he'd fallen short. Sadness joined them each night, an unwelcomed guest that attacked his soul. Despite his feigned joy, he could not shake the dark mood following him. While Maria watched with hopeful, helpful, loving patience, he'd fought to find his old self. But each day rolled into the next, one malaise-filled day after another.

But today was different because Jake had a secret. He knew what awaited him when he got home. He and Maria had been discussing it for months, a painful point of contention for a couple who rarely fought.

Maria said it was time.

She who had loved Bull as deeply, and had mourned with equal heart-wrenching pain, somehow found the strength to recover earlier. She told Jake it was time they brought a dog back into their home.

No, it wouldn't . . . couldn't be the same. No, there would never be another like . . . but it was time. They loved dogs and wanted their children to grow up with the love and responsibility of a dog.

He'd finally agreed the time had come, so now Jake knew when he got home tonight, he would once again return to a home with a dog.

At first, Maria hadn't understood why he didn't want to join the family when they went to the shelter to pick their newest member. Then she did. Jake had made his choice as a young boy and could never repeat that moment of exquisite pleasure. No, it was time for others who would remember that perfect moment for a lifetime.

The decision made, she couldn't resist quoting a few lines of Wordsworth to her English teacher husband, who so often used poetry to make his points.

She had stood next to Jake at the kitchen sink, the last dish dried and placed away in the cupboard, surrounded by the silence that comes to a young home only late at night when children sleep. She reached out, taking his hand, looked into his eyes, and recited:

Though nothing can bring back the hour
Of splendour in the grass,
of glory in the flower;
We will grieve not, rather find
Strength in what remains behind;

Jake sighed, again appreciating how lucky he was to have this woman in his life. This woman who knew him so well she could recite the lines that perfectly captured the emotions of this moment. It was a moment he had been building toward these last six months. Yes, he must celebrate and revel in what was left behind.

Maria pushed herself onto her toes, locked her fingers behind his neck, and slowly rose toward him, pulling Jake's face down to meet hers. Their lips met, joining them in a soulful kiss known only to a lucky few. The kiss offered the salt of their tears, but so much more.

Jake wiped away a tear. Yes, it was time to bring a dog back into their home, to let a dog back into his heart.

His classroom now empty, Jake reached for his briefcase, his lips curling upward as he turned to leave. Walking up the stairs to their small, well-lit home, he found the bounce back in his step. He was met at the door by a loving wife and two extraordinarily energetic and giggling children shouting: "We did it! We did it! His name is Bandit!"

Hiding behind the mayhem stood a slightly malnourished, soon-to-be-oversized, big-boned, skittish mutt, who watched Jake with frightened but ever-hopeful eyes.

"They found him on the streets foraging," Maria said. "They guess he's a little over six months old and has only known a feral existence. He might need some extra loving, but hey, who's better at that than this family? The folks at the shelter say he's smart as a whip and proven pretty adept at stealing food, hence the name."

Maria dropped to a knee and wrapped her arms around the anxious dog as she continued.

"It's funny, we went there intending to pick out a

dog, but it feels like he picked us. There were close to a hundred dogs. Some barking, some silently watching. But when we got to Bandit's cage, he looked right at me with the oddest expression. This may sound strange, but it felt like he gave me the stink-eye. Like he was saying: 'What took you so long?' Bandit held my gaze a few moments. Then, with his head up and tail high, he walked over calmly and stood at the front of the cage. He gave each of the kids a quick lick and sat down directly in front of me, like he'd been living with us for years and was waiting for me to get his leash for a walk."

Maria shook her head. "Yvonne at the shelter called it the darnedest thing. Until then, Bandit had been skittish around everyone. She said Bandit sat back, refusing to interact with the dozens of people who'd been in the past week. Isn't that unbelievable?"

Jake smiled, a knowing smile. He'd seen that very moment played out before, long ago. He exhaled, at peace, confident his family, and Bandit, had chosen well.

"Actually, it's totally believable, but it might take a review of fifteen thousand years of human and dog evolution for me to explain."

"Oh my!" Maria said, standing and brushing her lips against his. "Well, perhaps we'll wait and share this topic with our guests. Go wash up. Nonna Anna, Abuelo Tomás, and Uncle Diego will be here soon. I believe Uncle Diego is as excited about this new family member as any of us."

They had a wonderful dinner, a dinner like long ago, filled with joyful memories and bright hopes for the future. The family laughed and told stories while Bandit, fed and taken out to relieve himself, slowly slipped into a cautious, watchful rest. He grew relaxed enough that raised eyebrows as he followed people's movements around the room now sufficed. Slowly, his intense watchfulness faded, and the sounds from this noisy, loving family lulled him into an unfamiliar state of calm.

Hours later, the children in bed, their guests gone, Maria, wrapped in a blanket on the couch, slept. Jake returned from taking the dog on a long, somewhat frenetic walk as he discovered Bandit had yet to learn the nuances of the leash. But, no worries, it would come. He was a good boy. His family had done well.

Fixing the blanket on Maria, Jake gently brushed away the fallen hair from her face. Then, he turned away and walked to the corner of the room where his computer rested, silent. Jake hadn't written anything in months.

Through the years, he'd maintained a quixotic quest, searching for stories he believed worth telling. He'd had a few short stories appear in obscure online publications. But through it all, he'd struggled, searching for a particular story that touched his soul and he hoped might touch others. That story had proven more elusive than grasping smoke from a dying campfire. No plot, no storyline, no character, nothing seemed to resonate as palpable and real enough until perhaps now.

Jake sat down and opened his laptop only to find the dog, with the most self-assuredness displayed since arriving in their home earlier that day, followed him into the corner.

More content than he'd been in a very long time, Jake reached down to run his hand along the flank of the now-compliant dog. Bandit accepted the touch, deep-rooted and familiar, like the caress of an old friend, then stretched out with all four paws pressing against the wall, offering a self-assured sigh.

He tucked his feet under Bandit, and the dog's eyes fluttered as Jake sat motionless, searching for something that had eluded him for so long. Jake leaned forward, placed his fingers on the keyboard, and began to type.

I close my eyes, remembering the first time I ever saw the dog. The pup was in a large box lined with old towels, wrestling and playing with the others. I walked toward him as he attentively sniffed, cocked his head, looking above the lip of the box like he'd been expecting me.

I liked the look of him immediately and wanted to pick him up. The energetic pup made it easier for me. He stepped on the head of one littermate and nipped the ear of another to move closer. The dog pushed himself to the front so he could stand up like a human, his front paws scraping on the side of the box right in front of me. My parents' eyes darted from one puppy to the next, commenting on each. But I fixed only on this one and never turned away.

I looked down, and it was like I'd known him all my life. Even longer, if that were possible. I stared into his eyes, and he held my gaze like no other dog ever had. I reached into the box, picked him up, and brought him to my chest.

He was home.

It was strange. It felt like this dog had been waiting for me, and I had to take him home. He needed me, as I would him, and we would be there for each other. I, a young boy, and this special dog. I brought him close to my face. He gave me a couple of quick licks, and I saw strength and goodness in this dog that I wanted, no, needed. I didn't pull away or giggle, accepting the licks for what they were, a commitment to be my friend for life. My eyes shining bright, I looked up at my smiling parents, and words formed on my lips, words I'd never been surer of.

"He's the one."

A wet nose brushed Jake's hand as Bandit's chin came to rest on the desk. Jake smiled and reached out to run his hand across the dog's flank. Bringing his hands to the sides of the dog's head, he turned Bandit to face him.

"What do you think? Can I do justice to this story?"

Bandit studied him, the dog's presence filling Jake with calm. Jake stared into Bandit's liquid brown eyes, familiar and ancient, as the story of his life with Bull unfolded in his mind clearer than a cloudless arctic sky.

Jake leaned forward to give Bandit a warm embrace, and the now relaxed dog nuzzled to get closer as Jake wiped a solitary tear from his cheek.

After more than six months of heartache, Bandit had come into his life to deliver Bull's final gift, the story of their life together. Jake held Bandit even tighter, then sat back to look into the dog's knowing eyes.

"I won't let you down."

Made in the USA
Las Vegas, NV
03 December 2022